BUTCH II

BUTCH II

a novel by Jay Rayn

Boston ◆ Lace Publications

an imprint of Alyson Publications, Inc.

This book is dedicated to parents.
We are always your children.

Copyright © 1994 by Jay Rayn.
Cover photograph copyright © 1994 by Catherine Hopkins.

Typeset and printed in the United States of America.
Printed on recycled, acid-free paper.

This is a trade paperback from Lace Publications,
an imprint of Alyson Publications, Inc.,
40 Plympton Street, Boston, Massachusetts 02118.
Distributed in England by GMP Publishers,
P.O. Box 247, London N17 9QR, England.

First edition: May 1994

5 4 3 2 1

ISBN 1-55583-317-9

The text from *The Thorn Birds,* by Colleen McCuller, is taken
from the foreword, copyright © 1981 by Colleen McCuller.

The lyrics of "The Bandit," copyright © 1981 by Madeline Davis,
which appear on pp. 89–90, are reprinted by permission of the
composer.

Library of Congress Cataloging-in-Publication Data
Rayn, Jay, 1950–
    Butch II : a novel / by Jay Rayn. — 1st ed.
        p.   cm.
    ISBN 1-55583-317-9 (acid-free paper) : $8.95
    1. Lesbians—United States—Fiction.   I. Title.
PS3568.A935B82 1994
813'.54—dc20   94-1077
                                                                CIP

CONTENTS

ACKNOWLEDGMENTS

The author gratefully acknowledges the following: Madeline Davis for the use of her lyrics and history; Ana and Amalia for their presence and influence; Sue Tournour, Deb Siefert, and Joyce Cromwell for their critical reading. A special thanks to Julia Rayna for her devotion and enthusiasm.

MIKE
AGAIN

"Oh, she walks in boots of leather and slippers made of gold. She'll be a child forever, and forever she'll be old. She's the heroine of legends. She's the eagle and the dove. She's the daughter of the moon. She's my sister and my love."

Mike softly sang the words that confirmed her identity as she opened the door to her first-floor apartment. It was time for more changes. Her five-year relationship with Leslie was over, and Mike knew her life would never be the same.

She checked her closet to see which clothes she'd left at Leslie's and then emptied her dresser drawers to start sorting through her once-shared life. At first, she carefully folded the women's studies t-shirts that were Leslie's symbols of freedom. But, soon, she was angrily wadding them up and stuffing them into a paper bag. A part of her was still in love. A part of her would never love again.

Somewhere in the back of her broken heart she could hear a soft knock at her door. She didn't want Leslie's politically correct overtures of friendship right now. She didn't want to look at a face she had once adored and know that someone else was caressing it, kissing it, watching a reflection of shared love. She didn't want closeness or caring or talk or touches or anything that might cause more pain.

The knock came again. Mike's trembling hands crushed the paper bag. She assumed a belligerent stance by the door and prepared a glare. She turned the knob and then flung the door open so violently, it crashed off the wall.

"What?"

She stared into an empty hallway.

"Geez, Mike, I didn't mean to bother ya." Mike lowered her gaze to the tiny figure in front of her. Amalia's brown eyes were wide with fear, and her little fist held tightly to a cassette tape. "You left this upstairs. You know, the tape with the butch song on it. I didn't want it to get lost in all our junk."

"Thanks, squirt." Kneeling at Amalia's eye level, Mike gently reached out to touch her friend so that she wouldn't feel so threatened. "It's good to have someone looking out for my stuff," Mike said with a wink.

Amalia warmed quickly as she studied Mike's eyes. "I also came down for somethin' else. I didn't get my buddy squeeze this morning."

Mike put the bag and tape on the floor and opened her arms. Amalia's eyes twinkled with joy as she took two steps backward and then leaped into the hug she always asked for. Squeezing Amalia tightly, Mike spun around until they were both a little dizzy.

"That's more like it," Amalia said. "Now we can get down to business."

Amalia marched into the living room and took her favorite seat on Mike's wavy black chair.

"My mom's on the way to Women's Studies and she says you and I have the whole day together. What do ya think we should do?"

"Is she gone already?"

Amalia nodded.

"How long?"

"Don't know. It's Women's Studies and it's Saturday. She could be gone till midnight."

"Hmmm." Mike looked around at the scattered clothes and picture albums. "Wanna watch some television? I've got some things I have to do."

"Whatever," Amalia said. "I can even help if you want."

"Spanish or English?" Mike asked.

"English, please. The programs in Spanish are boring."

After turning on the set, Mike went back to the bedroom. She stuffed earrings, socks, sandals, posters, herbs, and teas into a bag and made a list of all the things Leslie needed to return to her, including photos, rings, and Marine Corps stuff. She'd drive by Leslie's late at night and leave the bag on the porch. It was safer that way.

"Hey, Mike! There's a commercial on about traveling half-price."

Mike smiled as she listened from the bedroom.

"The man says to call your travel agent right now and tell him you want a ticket on Koala, or something like that. Are you gonna call?"

Mike walked into the living room looking very serious. "Do you really think I should?"

"He says we should."

"But where am I going?"

"To Osmalia, or somethin'. It's half-price!"

Suddenly, Mike pretended to cry.

"What'sa matter, Mike?"

"I don't wanna go. I'd have to leave you here in Buffalo and I wouldn't see you anymore and I wouldn't get my daily squeeze and I wouldn't have anyone to look after me and—"

"Shhh. Don't cry, Mike. You don't have to go." Amalia stroked Mike's arm and patted her head. "You don't *have* to do what the man said. You can see me every day and I'll always give you a squeeze."

"Promise?"

"Promise. Cross my Chilean heart and hope to die."

"Don't hope to die, squirt," Mike said, hugging her. "Just cross your heart and leave it at that."

"Why do people do that anyway? Cross their hearts?"

The knot in Mike's chest tightened as she searched for an answer to Amalia's question. She remembered crossing

9

her heart when she had promised to always love Sharon, her first girlfriend. She had crossed her heart when Leslie had asked her to never stop touching her.

"Maybe it's because people don't really listen to their hearts," Amalia said with a wisdom only children have. "When you cross it, your fingers are kinda tying it down and marking the spot so you always know where it is. If you tie your heart down, you have to listen to it."

Mike tenderly pushed Amalia's shiny black hair away from her eyes. She loved her. At times, Mike felt like the father Amalia didn't have. She wanted to take her in her lap and tell her all the things a father might to make life a little easier. Amalia's dimpled smile always made the day more important, and Mike felt proud whenever Amalia's trusting hand was in hers.

But even Amalia couldn't make the pain of losing Leslie disappear. Every morning Mike remembered. Every night she cried. She couldn't make their breakup seem final. Leslie was alive and living a few blocks away. She was having parties, making plans, and loving someone else. She wasn't dead and gone forever. Mike couldn't miss her without anger, and she couldn't hate her without pain. It was time to grow.

❏ ❏

Mike checked in at the health spa, confident that a stronger body would erase unwanted memories. She wore a t-shirt and jeans, and had decided she'd even wear shorts if she had to, though it meant exposing her once-crippled legs for all to see. While she waited for an attendant, Mike watched men of all sizes preen and pump. Long-haired women stood around the gym chatting as if the men were in charge of their physical futures.

"We have to measure you on the first day," the sales attendant said, "to see how many inches you lose over time. Do you know your measurements?"

Mike shook her head.

"Well, how about your bra size?"

"Don't wear one."

"Girdle?"

"Nope."

The attendant looked puzzled as she measured Mike's wrist. "How about stockings?" She searched Mike's smiling eyes for an answer.

"I wear size eight socks," Mike said.

"Oh. Uh, no bra, huh?"

Mike shook her head again.

"But you look ... I mean your, uh, your chest doesn't bounce or ... you work out much?"

"Not yet." Pressing the palms of her hands together, Mike flexed her chest muscles. "Just strong pecs. My mother used to hate it when I flexed like this."

The attendant held back a laugh as Mike flexed alternate pecs. She blushed when she reached around Mike's waist with the tape measure.

"Can you push the top of your jeans down a little? The belt's a little thick and..."

"No problem. Let me take it off for ya."

Mike slowly removed the belt with the Marine Corps buckle and jerked her jeans down onto her hips. "Want me to take off my shirt? Would that make it easier?"

After flashing a glance at Mike's chest, the attendant got very busy measuring Mike's waist.

"No ... no, I think we can do it ... We usually do it over clothes. You can keep your shirt on, and your slacks, I mean jeans ... pants! Oh, I'm sorry. I think it's been a long day or something."

Smiling supportively, Mike raised her arms so the attendant could reach all the way around.

"Twenty-four. Now the hips."

Mike wanted to flex her butt muscles, but she was starting to feel a little sorry for the attendant.

"Thirty-five. Now the, uh ... Can you raise your arms again, please?"

The tape slid up and down Mike's chest as the attendant nervously tried to find the right spot.

"Finally! Thirty-six. Okay, we got it. Now, can you raise your pant leg so I can measure your calf?"

Mike willingly obeyed. This was obviously a much safer area. Mike watched for the attendant's reaction to her unshaven leg.

"Flexed or unflexed?" Mike asked.

"It's fine the way it is. I'm done. I mean, we're done."

Mike could almost hear a thank-you as the attendant sighed and wiped her brow.

"What was it, exactly, that you wanted to work on?"

"Everything," Mike said with a mischievous smile. "I just wanna get stronger and healthier. You know, look good, stuff like that."

Mike knew her flirting was flustering the attendant. "Guess I'll go change." She couldn't hold back a wink as she grabbed her gym bag and headed for the locker room.

She shyly changed into shorts and a tank top while making sure she didn't inadvertently stare at the seminaked women walking past her. She felt stares as she hopped on the stationary bike to sweat away her past. But once she started pedaling, they didn't matter. She was ten again and riding her bike in the wind. This was her horse. She could escape. She could be a knight in shining armor. She pedaled faster, bending over the handlebars to cut down imaginary wind resistance. She was Zorro and Wild Bill Hickok. She felt alive and gallant. There was Sharon, her first and forever love. She'd scoop her up onto her horse and ride off into the sunset. There was Leslie and her new lover. She pulled her six-gun and shot them as she sped past. There was the ocean of the far West. She slowed her horse, remembering Sue.

Mike was alone again. Her horse was just a bike. She glared at the people around her to make them look away. She liked being alone. Almost. It seemed she had been in some kind of relationship every day since Sharon. Sixteen of her twenty-nine years. Ana and Amalia were her family now. But Ana was no lover: she was a straight Chilean with a Moslem boyfriend. Mike wanted to keep her distance. She'd ride alone for a while.

❑ ❑

She finished five miles on the bike and then checked her knees for swelling. Her scars from the Marines would always be with her. The stares subsided as Mike moved to a biceps machine. Everyone was getting involved in their own bending and shaping. Mike glanced at a tall, seemingly strong

12

woman and knew right away she had to be gay. She wished there was some kind of signal lesbians could give each other so they wouldn't have to guess. She decided the three-finger Girl Scout sign might work if she spread the fingers so no one would think she was actually a Scout. It could symbolize the three points of a pink triangle. She transferred her weights to one hand and waited for the tall woman to look her way. When they made eye contact, Mike tapped her chest three times. The woman smiled and seemed to nod in understanding. They returned to their workouts, keeping an occasional eye on each other.

Suddenly, Mike heard a deep, throaty voice behind her.

"Hello! Aren't you Mike? Mike Landetti? Leslie's ex?"

Mike didn't turn around. She continued pumping her biceps as she answered.

"I guess that's one way to describe me," she said. "It seems we're only known by who we're with now or by who we used to be with."

"It's Maggie," the voice said. "Maggie Romano."

Dropping the weights to her sides, Mike quickly turned around.

"I'm a little ... out of breath," Maggie said before spraying medicine from an inhaler into her mouth. "Asthma. I just started this ridiculous program."

Mike scanned Maggie's large body with a sensuous smile. Though Mike had met her before and seen her perform at parties, Maggie seemed bigger than Mike remembered her. She was at least six inches taller than Mike. Most people would probably say she needed to lose at least a hundred pounds, but Mike thought she was a woman born to be big. All of her parts seemed to fit.

"I don't think you even have to be here," Mike said. "You look fine to me."

Maggie chuckled and loudly cleared her throat. "We're about done. Would you like to join us in the pool?"

Smiling widely, the tall woman snaked her way through the gym to Maggie's side. Mike tried to stand tall. Putting her hands on her hips, she rocked from heel to toe.

"I'll meet you there," Mike said, almost defiantly. Watching them leave together, she again felt the stares of those around her. She grabbed a towel and nonchalantly strolled around the workout room.

"Lookin' good," she said to a blonde woman. To a young redheaded woman who needed no more work she said, "Keep tryin'. Don't give up." She made an ugly face at an egocentric, bare-chested man and put the towel up to her mouth as if she were going to be sick. She hated that men could bare their chests and often tried to embarrass them when they did.

After changing to a clean t-shirt, she headed for the pool. She had never worn a women's bathing suit and wasn't going to start now. The pool area was shared by men and women all trying to impress each other, and of course, Mike looked like no one else. She searched for Maggie, walked in and out of the whirlpool to get wet, and tried very hard to look like she knew why she was there. She finally gave up and went to the showers, but when she saw the open stalls and naked wet women, she decided to leave and shower at home. She dressed quickly and raced to the parking lot.

"We couldn't wait," Maggie said from her car window. "Maybe we'll see you next time. We come three times a week."

Mike just nodded and waved as the car drove away. Seeing the tall woman in the passenger seat confused Mike. She had thought the woman was a butch, but no butch would let a femme drive her around. It was almost her duty to be the driver. Dads drive, mothers ride. Butches drive, femmes ride. She knew Maggie was a femme. She had responded immediately to her flirtation. Mike also knew by listening to all the songs Maggie had written and sung, that Maggie knew butches like only a femme could. Mike concluded that the tall woman must also be a femme and that the two of them were buddies.

❏ ❏

Ana and Amalia were in the black chair watching television when Mike got home. She had grown accustomed to leaving her door unlocked so that they could have access to her apartment and the material things they didn't have.

"Ah, so you're back," Ana said with a smile. "Are you stronger? Let me check."

"Ha-ha," Mike said. She was used to Ana teasing her about her body.

Ana cupped Mike's face in her hands. "You look good," she said gently. "Don't feel guilt about Leslie. Her life is her own, and she decided. Trying to be tougher won't change anything."

Mike tried to look away, but Ana held her face.

"We love you. Amalia adores you. There's no need to change who you are."

Mike half smiled. After a moment of searching each other's eyes, Ana lightly slapped her cheek.

"Okay. So now we understand each other. Can you help me with my daughter? When she falls asleep like this I can't wake her up, and she's too big now for me to carry her."

Mike quietly lifted Amalia into her arms and felt that special warmth that comes with a child's natural love. "Good thing I'm getting tougher and stronger," she said.

Ana only smiled and led the way up the three flights of stairs to her apartment. Together, they put Amalia to bed and removed her shoes and socks. Together, they covered her. Together, they stood at the door watching her sleep. Mike automatically put an arm around Ana's shoulders. She was surprised when Ana didn't move away.

"Where's Bill?" Mike asked when they finally moved to the kitchen.

"He's not coming tonight."

"Home with one of the wives?"

Ana shrugged and Mike felt bad that she had asked. "Got any coffee?"

They sat knee to knee at the table. Through the night, they played word games and talked about broken hearts and laughed and sat in understanding silence. A few times, Ana's hand touched hers and Mike felt a familiar excitement growing inside of her. Each time Ana touched her, she pulled away. Each time, pulling away got harder.

"I need to go home," Mike said.

"If you want."

"I don't want, I need."

"Uh-huh. What do you need?"

15

Standing, Mike stuffed her hands in her pockets. "I don't know what I need. I just think I should go home."

"Then you should go," Ana said. She led Mike to the door without another word.

"Thanks," Mike said. "I'll see you tomorrow."

When Mike was halfway down the hallway, she turned to look back at Ana's door.

"Call me when you know what you want," Ana said.

❏ ❏

Mike sat silently on her couch until sunrise. Ana's words always confused her. When the phone rang at 7 a.m., an alarm went off in Mike's heart. She suffered through a dozen rings before finally answering it.

"Can you give Amalia a ride to school? She missed her bus."

"Okay," Mike said. "Send the squirt down in five minutes."

"Can you come and get her?"

Mike was too tired to argue. After tapping on Ana's door, she knelt to await Amalia's morning squeeze. As if on cue, Amalia leaped into her arms. Ana nodded a thank-you as Amalia took Mike's hand.

"I knew you'd be awake," Ana said as she closed her door.

After dropping Amalia off, Mike rushed home to shower and get ready for her job at the university. The car radio was playing Gloria Gaynor as Mike parked, and the words "I will survive" stuck in her head. She was single now. She tried to scribble out Leslie's name everywhere she had doodled it on her desk blotter. As the day went on, she found herself looking at the women in the computer center as if for the first time.

She was friendlier than she'd ever been, almost too friendly. She catered to the secretaries in other offices and desperately tried to have conversations with anyone who had the time. A woman she didn't know, a student at the university, put a fruit salad on her desk and left with only a smile. Her ever-present pager went off just before quitting time and her heart jumped a little when she heard the voice.

"We're having a dinner party. Amalia said to invite you. Six o'clock. See you!"

Being with Ana and Amalia both excited and scared her. Arriving home, she cautiously checked her apartment to make sure it was empty and then locked the door behind her. She needed some time alone. She was sorting through her mail when she saw a letter from her mother. She panicked.

It was the first time her mother had ever written her. Though her mother had kicked her out at thirteen, Mike never completely hated her. She visited her parents once or twice a year and called once every three months. Secretly, she wished everything could have been different. Somewhere inside, she loved both her parents, but she couldn't be herself around them. She couldn't talk to them about the pain or joy in her life, and when they did speak to each other, there was always a tension that couldn't be broken.

Her mother was a stranger. She couldn't remember a kind word between them, only the yelling, the slaps, the baby-sitters, and the condemnation.

When Mike opened the letter, she was a little glad to see it was a short one.

Dear Michaelene,

I found this in a book I just read called The Thorn Birds and I could only think of you.

"There is a legend about a bird which sings just once in its life, more sweetly than any other creature on the face of the earth. From the moment it leaves the nest it searches for a thorn tree, and does not rest until it has found one. Then, singing among the savage branches, it impales itself upon the longest, sharpest spine. And, dying, it rises above its own agony to outcarol the lark and the nightingale. One superlative song, existence the price. But the whole world stills to listen, and God in His heaven smiles. For the best is only bought at the cost of great pain ... Or so says the legend."

You are my daughter and I bore you with great pain, but I'm afraid of your search for the thorn bush. Come home someday. Your song was always the sweetest.

Mom

Though she wasn't exactly sure what her mother was saying or why she was saying it, Mike felt the tears in her eyes and quickly wiped them away. She stuffed the letter in a drawer, promising to decipher it later when she felt more able, and then dressed in her traditional black shirt and blue jeans. She took a deep breath before knocking on Ana's door.

"Why are you knocking? Come in. Come in!"

Loud Latin music filled the small apartment as the guests, mostly Chileans, danced and laughed. Somehow, Mike didn't feel out of place. Amalia waved and got busy pretending to be a hostess. Ana went right back to dancing. Mike tried to smile at the strangers she passed, but her grin turned to a glare when she came face-to-face with Bill in the kitchen. Snickering arrogantly, he bobbed his head to the music as if this were his party and his house.

Mike made a sandwich and then leaned against the kitchen doorway with her back to Bill. She had never spoken to him, but she knew she didn't like him. Ana, still dancing, occasionally smiled toward the kitchen. When Mike caught Bill waving back to her, she decided it was time to make her move. After getting into the rhythm of the music, she took Ana's hand to spin her around. Soon, they were in the middle of a circle with everyone clapping. Ana was obviously pleased. When Mike started to tire, Ana pulled her back and made her keep dancing. Finally, the music ended, and they collapsed. Mike unbuttoned her shirt to the middle of her chest and used a towel to wipe away her sweat.

"I told you!" Ana said. "You have Latin blood! Here. A special necklace I made." She put it over Mike's head and tapped the silver against Mike's chest. "It will give you power."

Everyone continued dancing through the night. Mike put Amalia to bed without Ana noticing. Soon, only a few people in quiet conversation remained. Bill maintained his seat in the kitchen, and Mike was glad that no one really spoke or paid any attention to him. When Ana closed the door on the last of her guests, Mike took a seat on the couch next to the kitchen door and waited to see who would win. Ana played right along. She busied herself cleaning up the kitchen table and then spent the same amount of time with Mike in the living room. Bill and Mike glared at each other when Ana wasn't looking.

Finally, Bill gave up. He acted as if he had won when he swaggered toward the door, but Mike was the one left with Ana. She felt her power. After Ana closed the door, Mike stood to face her. Without hesitation, they walked into each other's arms. The passion they wanted to share was also a barrier as they held each other with only a breath between them. Slowly, they would almost kiss. Slowly, they would back away.

"I don't need you," Mike whispered.

"I know." Ana rubbed her cheek against Mike's as they held each other tighter.

After minutes of just feeling each other, Mike whispered again. "I want you."

Ana held Mike's face in her hands and then brushed back her hair with long fingernails. "I know."

It was a kiss Mike felt she had been waiting for forever. Ana's passion dug into her as they devoured each other. Ana knew how to give Mike just enough to make her want more. They knelt while their mouths explored and their hands grabbed at clothes and flesh. Once or twice, Mike wanted to stop. She wasn't ready for love again. But her heart pounded and Ana's rhythm was hers. She couldn't stop. She crossed over to a place she knew she'd never escape. With renewed energy, she explored Ana's mouth and slowly, deliberately, unbuttoned Ana's blouse. When her hand brushed Ana's tiny breast, Mike connected with that part of herself she knew was butch. She would caress, love, enjoy, and please the woman beneath her. And with each touch, each loving kiss, each bit of giving, she would please herself.

Their bodies swayed and danced as they stretched out on the floor. Ana removed Mike's shirt carefully, as if she knew that Mike's modesty and pride would battle each other. Mike felt her sensitivity and she helped Ana pull the shirt from her back. Now their sweat could mingle and blend. When Ana reached for Mike's belt, Mike distracted her by flicking her tongue on her nipples, caressing her hips, and massaging her flesh until Ana's body reached for her.

"Te amo, my bootch. *Mucho te amo."*

Mike felt the words tear at her very core. Each word, each sigh, each urgent moan ripped away the part of her heart that had once belonged to Leslie. Her heart cried, her soul screamed, and violently, her body released in mutual pain and pleasure.

At daybreak, Mike awoke with Ana cradled in the crook of her arm. She felt happiness, but she wasn't sure it was real. She felt guilty, as if she had cheated on Leslie. She felt victorious over Bill and knew she could give Ana more than Bill ever could. She felt wanted and loved, needed and appreciated, scared and lonely.

When Ana opened her eyes, she looked at Mike in a new way, a way that made Mike want to bury her in her arms, to keep her, to protect her.

"I have to go back to Chile," Ana said bluntly. "My visa from my ex-husband has expired and I have to go back. We have forty days to love each other."

"What are you talking about?" Mike pulled away abruptly and instinctively put on her shirt. "Can't you renew it? Can't you get a new one? Can't you—"

"Shhh. Don't ask questions about things you can't understand. You are American. Americans can fix things quickly and expect things to be okay. I may be able to get a new one, but I first must return to Chile."

"But the junta," Mike said. "You've told me all these things about them. How can you go back?"

"Chiquitita, Chile is my country, my people. We deal with things differently." Ana gently pushed Mike back down to the floor and laid her head on Mike's chest. "Hold me for a moment and then I'll make you a Chilean breakfast."

Mike held her and stroked her head, making sure Ana couldn't see her fear. Visions of the Chilean coup, of the junta, of torture and death terrified her. She frantically searched her mind for a solution.

❏ ❏

Mike spent the first days of winter researching libraries and bookstores for every bit of information about Chile she could find. She rushed home for dinner and playtime with Amalia, then spent hours questioning Ana about the coup, the country, her family.

"You must see the history," Ana would tell her, "then feel the plight of the people in your heart. Use your third eye to understand."

Mike studied photos from Santiago, Valparaiso, and Viña del Mar. She read documents by people who had evidenced the terror. She listened to the music of the fallen Victor Jara. She had once seen a mural in Oakland that featured only a musician's hands, hands torn from a body but still playing in the minds of a people. Victor Jara was a national hero because his music spoke to the people and he had died because of it.

"You can't speak about it, and there are things you can never tell," said Ana. "There is still danger. Those who study or work at the university are considered extremists and very dangerous. Those who work for unions are thought to be murderers. Many have died. Many are missing."

Mike spoke to attorneys about visas. She learned that Ana could stay in the United States only if she found a job for which no other American qualified.

Every night, Mike carried Amalia up the three flights of stairs. Every morning, she awoke to their smiles.

With only three weeks left before Ana had to leave, Mike decided to accept the inevitable and work on getting them back to the U.S. once they returned to Chile. She bought a Native American ring that she knew Ana would love and made a special bouquet of flowers for Amalia. Then she waited proudly at their door.

"Amalia, these are for you." She knelt on one knee to present the flowers, but Amalia didn't jump into her arms or even smile. After opening the door wider so Mike could come in, she silently retreated to her bedroom.

Mike slowly scanned the room to see what was wrong. When she saw the man's jacket on the couch and the rumpled covers on Ana's bed, she threw the flowers on the floor and slammed the door behind her. Amalia came out of the apartment and followed her down the hallway. Mike could hear her keeping her distance on the stairs.

"Might as well go home, kid. I'm not goin' in there right now."

When she stopped to listen for a reply, she instead heard Amalia crying.

"Shit," Mike whispered to herself. "Good work, Landetti. Take it out on the kid."

She climbed the stairs to the landing and sat next to her littlest friend. After a moment, she felt Amalia's fingers reaching for her. Together, they pretended to tap-dance down the stairs and then ran from the building hand in hand.

"Eat your ice cream, honey. We have to get back before your mother gets worried."

"No hurry."

Mike picked at her hot fudge trying to make designs in the melting ice cream.

"Which one are you mad at?" Mike asked without a glance.

"Mad at her, hate him," Amalia said, stabbing at her chocolate mountain. "Which one are you mad at?"

"Ditto, kid."

"Are you and Mom gonna fight now?"

"It'll probably be just me doing the fighting. Your mom will only smile and sing something in Spanish."

"Can I stay at your house tonight?"

"Nope. Running away doesn't work."

"Then why did *you* run away?"

Mike wet her napkin with the tip of her tongue and wiped some chocolate from the corner of Amalia's mouth.

"You're right. It's time to go," Mike said. "You pay and I'll meet ya at the door."

"Me?"

"Yup. Here's five. Three for the ice cream and two for your allowance."

"Oh yeah." Amalia smiled. "I forgot I get an allowance now."

"But only if you get home in time to help with the dishes."

"Okay. But only if *you* get there in time for coffee."

"Deal."

❏ ❏

Mike opened Ana's door with a flourish and a smile. Amalia ran to Ana's arms.

"So you're back," Ana said to Mike coldly. "Do you expect my whole life to change because of you?"

"Just a part of it," Mike said, still smiling. "Got any coffee?"

Ana gently pushed Amalia aside. "You Americans are all alike. He is in my life. You are in my life. Why can't you accept that?"

Mike picked up a coffee cup that she assumed was Bill's and dangled it from her finger.

"You know," Mike said, trying to hold in her anger, "every time that mealy-pricked son of a bitch comes around, you start in on me about being an American." Her Marine Corps pride rose to the surface, followed closely by her Italian temper. "What the hell do you have against Americans?"

"You know."

"No, I don't know. You've lived here, worked here. Your kid goes to school here. What the hell did we ever do to you?"

"So. You studied Chile. Did you learn about where the junta learned their torture? Do you remember the training camps in Panama and Texas?"

Mike's glare softened as she felt the guilt of American involvement. She lowered her eyes, feeling lost somewhere between her memories of Vietnam and her visions of a land she didn't know. She could barely hear Ana's voice as images of the military clouded her thoughts.

"Do you remember the rapes?" Ana continued. "We thought only American soldiers could do such things. We cried for the women of Vietnam. Then we cried for our sisters and our friends as the soldiers of Chile and Brazil did the same to them. Soldiers trained by Americans."

"I didn't train them," Mike whispered. "You can't hate all of us."

Ana relaxed her stance and softly touched Mike's arm. "I love you," she said. "But you are American. You have to take responsibility for the things America does."

Mike turned away from Ana's eyes as she quietly set the coffee cup back on the table. "There were Americans killed, too," she said. "Frank Terrugi, and the Hathaway guy. They

23

were tortured. They were lied about. The junta killed them."

Ana's grip tightened on Mike's arm. "And who trained the junta? And whose embassy lied about the killing? Why is Rockefeller Avenue in the heart of Santiago?"

Mike pulled away from Ana's grip and once again picked up the cup. "And who fills your head with lies in this house? Who makes you hate so much? Who makes you lie to me?"

She threw the cup across the kitchen, where it smashed against the wall. From somewhere behind her, she heard an almost silent scream. She turned to see tears in Amalia's eyes. Eyes that should have been filled with wonder and love and life were instead clouded with hate and anger and such terrible hurt. Pushing aside the broken pieces of glass, Mike knelt on the floor to reach Amalia. Ana knelt beside her and slowly, cautiously, put an arm around Mike's shoulders as Ana, too, reached for Amalia. The three of them huddled. Mike and Amalia cried while Amalia cuddled in Mike's lap like a child much younger than she was. The three of them touched and smiled and cried some more until Amalia escaped into sleep. Mike carefully took the Native American ring from her pocket and placed it in Ana's hand to seal their bond.

TO CHILE

Mike had just finished putting tinsel on the seven-foot Christmas tree that crowded the best corner of her apartment when Amalia breezed through the door.

"Wait, squirt! Wait!" Mike jumped off the footstool and spread her arms to block Amalia's view. "Turn around. I'm not ready yet."

Amalia obeyed. Mike smiled as she watched the little body shake in anticipation. After plugging in the string of four hundred lights, Mike darkened the rest of the room and waited for Amalia's reaction.

Amalia's eyes widened, and her hands opened and closed as if she were trying to touch each part of every branch.

"Good enough, kid?"

Amalia could only shake her head as she continued gazing in amazement. Mike wrapped her arms around her from behind. "I love Christmas trees. Especially when the lights fill up eyes like yours."

"It's the best tree I've ever seen, Mike."

"Better than any you've ever had?"

"I've never had one before."

"Well, I'll tell you what," Mike said, breaking off the tiny end of one branch, "since you like to save things so much, here's your own special branch to hide away so you can always remember."

"Oh, Mike. I'll put it in my special book, right next to the computer picture you drew me."

"That reminds me. There's something else I wanna give ya now so I won't forget."

Mike ran to her bedroom and searched her dresser drawer. Her mother's crumpled letter caught her eye, and she stuffed it in her pocket. After more hunting, she found the picture she was looking for.

"Remember this? Your mother took this picture at the park. Me and you freezing on the swing! I want you to keep it with you, and if you ever need me, like in an emergency or something, look at this picture and think real hard. I'll be right beside you."

Amalia held the picture in one hand and the branch in the other as she threw her arms around Mike's neck.

"And don't forget," Mike said. "Christmas Eve, my house, okay?"

"Deal!"

❏ ❏

Mike borrowed money from the bank and shopped as she never had before. She wanted Amalia to have everything she'd asked for, but she had to make sure it could all be packed and carried to Chile. With the utmost care she bought a Buffalo t-shirt, a small microscope, a tape recorder, and Magic Markers. Later, she added a suitcase, a few records, a diary, and a photo album to the growing list. So that she could surprise Amalia on Christmas Eve, Mike hid the wrapped presents all over her apartment. She told Ana about some of the gifts but kept the others secret.

Five days before Christmas, she took Ana and Amalia to a fund-raising farewell party that Ana's friends had arranged. Ana needed the money to survive in Chile. Mike ignored her feelings for Bill so as not to ruin the party. When it was over, Ana handed her twelve hundred dollars to keep until they could exchange it for traveler's checks.

"It's safest with you," Ana said. "Everyone knows you're an ex-Marine. They're afraid of you."

The next night, Ana invited Mike to dinner. She wanted some quiet time with just the three of them, especially as time was running out and people were constantly visiting to say good-bye. Ana and Mike played their normal word games and settled some details about leaving. After Amalia went to bed, they cuddled for hours on the couch, barely speaking.

"I'll get you back," Mike said. "No matter what, I'll get you back." She repeated it again and again as they spent their last few hours alone together.

At 2 a.m., more Chilean friends knocked at the door to drop things off they wanted delivered to their homeland. A letter here, a package there. Each time someone went back, she or he became a courier. When Mike couldn't keep up with the Spanish anymore, she patted Ana on the shoulder and left. They'd still have Christmas Eve.

When Mike got to her hallway, she silently yelled at Amalia for leaving her door open and the lights on.

"The kid watches too much television," she said to herself.

But the sight that greeted her at her apartment doorway made her jump back. She felt like running away while yelling as loudly as she could, but instead, she charged in, adrenaline pumping. Everything but the furniture was gone. She cracked her neck to make sure she was awake. She checked the apartment number to be sure she had the right place.

Beer cans with cigarette butts crushed out on top of them were neatly placed against the wall. From the door, Mike could see all of her apartment except the bathroom and one side of the kitchen. The stereo, the television, lamps, radios, and her tape recorder were gone. She squinted into her bedroom, then cautiously stepped in to turn on the light. Her drawers were emptied on her bed. Books and papers were torn. Her file cabinet was pried open and everything from inside was either missing or in pieces.

She searched for the phone, half expecting to find it gone, too.

"Ana? Come down. There's trouble."

After hanging up, she went back out into the hallway. She felt attacked and violated. She couldn't stand to be in the emptiness. When she heard Ana's footsteps on the stairs, she didn't move. She couldn't move. She could only stand and look through the doorway.

Sensing danger, Ana approached the door cautiously.

"Oh, my God. My God! Who could do this?"

She took Mike by the hand and led her through the rooms. Mike had to look away. She noticed pine needles on the wood floor and followed them out her door and down the long hallway to the outer foyer. The presents were gone. The hidden special gifts for Amalia were gone. Everything from under the tree had been taken. Even the tree looked bruised and battered, as if it had put up a struggle against its attackers.

"I have to get back to my guests, Mike. Call the super. And the police. I'll check with you soon."

With that, she gave Mike a peck on the cheek and left her standing alone.

"Hey, Peter, what happened, man?"

Tony, the superintendent for the entire complex, always called her Peter. He said it was because he could never remember Mike's name and because she constantly had beautiful women around. The best name he could remember was Peter. He found her sitting in the hallway with her head on her knees. She gestured toward her door. "Oh, no, man. Oh, no. Who did this, Peter? Do you know who did it? Oh, man. We got to call the cops, Peter. Did you call 'em yet?"

Mike managed a nod but couldn't find the energy to get up. "They went right out the front door, Tony. They left a trail of pine needles. Someone had to see them. They went right out the front door."

Tony checked the apartment door and then looked at Mike in confusion. "Were you here? Were you inside, Peter?"

Mike shook her head.

"Well then, how'd they get in? You have your door locked?"

Again Mike shook her head. "I leave it open so the kid can watch TV."

"Oh, no. You can't be doin' things like that. Look. I'll go check with people who might still be up. You wait here for the cops, okay? You be all right, now. Man, you shoulda locked your door."

The police told her to take an inventory of everything. It was good she had large furniture, they said, or that would have been gone, too. They hoped she had insurance and told her that from now on, she should lock her door. And too bad about Christmas, they said, but it was the season for this kind of thing.

Mike sorted through the mess while she waited for Ana's return. Something didn't feel right. The living room was left empty, but neat. The bedroom, however, looked like someone was searching for something specific. Every file, every high school yearbook, every photo album was torn or strewn across the room. Even letters from friends had been opened and methodically laid out under the piles of clothes on the bed. Mike knew this was more than an ordinary burglary. She flashed on past images of investigations in the Marine Corps.

A knock at the door startled her. She hadn't expected Ana back so soon.

"Don't worry," she said as she started to open the door. "They didn't get the money—"

"It's me, Peter. That's good they didn't get the money."

"Sorry, Tony. I thought you were someone else."

"Yeah, I know. You thought I was one of your lady friends, right?"

"I guess so."

"Well, Peter. I checked with everyone and no one saw nothin'."

"They had to be in here for some time, Tony. They drank a lot of beer. It's almost as if they knew exactly how long I was going to be gone. Or like they had someone watching so they knew when I was coming back. I was right upstairs the whole time."

"Well, all I know is it's no one from in here. It ain't no inside job. Uh-uh. None of these people would do something like this."

Mike suddenly remembered the Air Force jacket that had once belonged to her father. She quickly checked behind the

29

bedroom door. When she saw the empty hook, she started to shake.

"They took the only thing my father ever gave me," she said. "The only damn thing I ever got from my family."

Respecting Mike's pain, Tony silently left the apartment. Mike ripped a blanket from her bed, hurling debris into the air, and cuddled into a fetal position on the couch. Ana's money was tucked safely in her front pocket and she'd somehow find a way to give them Christmas, but now she needed rest. She knew Ana was too busy to come back down, so she closed her eyes and tried to sleep away her pain.

She dreamt of her father as a young man. He was one of five Italian brothers, all in uniform and ready to die for their country. He swaggered and smiled in her dream, and the girls he passed on the street called him "Fast Al." He wore his pilot's jacket everywhere until the time came for him to turn in his uniform for a double-breasted suit. The jacket went into mothballs and Mike's dream turned into a nightmare. She could see his angry fist coming toward her head, her stomach, any part of her he could strike. She ducked and ran and tried to scream so he would stop hitting her. She ran down Main Street in Fredonia and through the cemetery to Sharon's house. She knocked and knocked, pleading for someone to save her, but it was Mike's mother, not Sharon, who opened the door. Her fiery red hair blew in the wind and she wore the pilot's jacket. Mike could see her father chasing after her as her mother blocked her way. Finally, with an eerie smile, her mother handed her a letter. As she took it, she could see the growing hand of her father crashing against her head. She threw her body to the floor.

Mike awoke panting, sweating, and shivering. She stumbled through the clutter and out the door. She raced down the hallway, still covered with pine needles, and burst through the outer door and into the snow. Only when she had reached her car did she slow enough to breathe. She unconsciously locked her car doors and turned on the heater to warm herself. Slowly, she pulled her mother's letter from her pocket. Squinting through her cold sweat, she read it once, then again, and again. The sun rose on glittering snow as she tore the letter into tiny pieces and tossed them out the window.

❏ ❏

She arrived at work a different person. She could feel that once-familiar armor shielding her again. She would protect herself and survive. She worked into the early evening. She was in no hurry to get home. A fruit salad mysteriously appeared on her desk. She had phone messages from Leslie and Ana, even one from Maggie Romano; she returned no calls. She went to the health spa to be alone, but when she saw Maggie's car, she spun on the ice and raced away. She drove the hour to Fredonia through a soft snowfall and silently parked in front of Sharon's house. Christmas lights lined the streets and there was a gentle silence in the small town. She walked from Sharon's to Maple Avenue, where her parents still lived, and strode past their house with hardly a glance. Memories of the town slowly filled her with the warmth of the season. She said a silent "Merry Christmas" to Sharon and blew her a kiss, then drove back to the city, calmer and ready to give again.

On Christmas Eve, her house was clean and filled with carols from a new stereo. Duplicate presents were wrapped and waiting for the child in her life. Amalia opened them quietly, smiling sweetly at each one. Mike watched Ana for approval, but all three of them seemed lost in their thoughts. On Christmas Day, Ana and Amalia would be on their way to Chile. Though they tried to share and love and enjoy their last night together, they could only pretend. The emptiness was already upon them. As if practicing for the time to come, no one's eyes met when they said good-bye at the door.

Mike retreated to the city's snow-covered streets. She wandered aimlessly on this most special of nights. She wished there were carolers. She hoped to hear church bells. Instead, she found others with no place to go. To each, she offered coffee or a Christmas greeting. She promised herself that from now on, she would always do this. Any Christmas Eve she could, she would find the people who most needed a friend.

By morning, Ana's hallway was filled with all the people who wanted to be special in her eyes. Each had a sense of their own importance and each hurried to be the center of attention. Mike was a silent observer. Amalia's eyes searched the floor as she patiently sat on an overstuffed suitcase. Ana raced from one person to the next, making sure all ends were tied and all ties were broken. When it was time for the caravan to leave for the airport, Mike went downstairs to wait behind her apartment door. She and Ana had agreed that no one could know how deeply they cared for each other. They would say good-bye alone.

Amalia came first. Though Mike tried to lift her chin to look in her eyes, Amalia steadfastly avoided her gaze. Instead, she gave Mike the hardest squeeze of her life. It was then that Mike felt the life within her drain away. Amalia pulled away abruptly and ran down the hall. Mike barely had strength enough to close her door. She leaned her forehead against the wall as she waited for the final knock. It came quietly, and all of Mike's fears and anxieties and love and need exploded as she pulled Ana to her.

"I'll always love you," she cried. "I'll get you back."

"Me too," Ana gasped. "Me too."

They kissed a final kiss, and hugged in final urgency. Then Ana was gone. Mike wrapped herself in her own arms and stood trembling by the door.

Once more she whispered, "I'll get you back."

❏ ❏

The snows of Buffalo were relentless that winter. January brought record-breaking temperatures, and Mike's body constantly ached from the gripping cold. She had wrapped herself in blankets to sit through New Year's Eve. Every morning, she shook as she wrote letters to Ana and Amalia. One letter could take up to a month to arrive. Often, they were censored or mysteriously lost. Still, she wrote at least once a day; sometimes, three or four.

She bought vitamins to fight off the cold and often stayed home from work to avoid the weather. After two weeks, she could no longer stand her complete isolation. Maggie and the tall woman, who to Mike's confusion had turned out to be Maggie's butch lover, invited Mike to join them at the spa. She forced herself to comply. It would be safer being with a couple. If she inadvertently flirted, it wouldn't be misunderstood. There'd be no assumptions or games. They could build a friendship. Many of Mike's friends had taken sides during her breakup with Leslie; others had moved away to start careers or be closer to lovers. The community of the seventies was gone, often divided and self-destructive.

Maggie joined Mike at the stationary bikes and moaned and complained about the necessity of exercise.

"If I could just ... get this damn seat ... in the right position, maybe I could..."

"Here," Mike said. "I'll fix it for you."

"Oh, great. Thank you."

Mike held Maggie's elbow as she helped her up on the bike.

"Ahhh! There! Got it." Maggie finally settled in for a ride. Her dramatics about the whole thing made Mike smile.

"You're sure you're on?" Mike teased.

Maggie nodded, patting her chest as if already tiring.

"You could always ride sidesaddle," Mike said. "I don't know how girls ever did that, but maybe it's easier to get on that way."

"If it were a horse I'd think about it, but you'll never catch me on a horse."

"I can catch anybody if they're on a horse," Mike smiled, slipping into a Groucho Marx imitation.

"No, I mean you wouldn't find me ... oh." Maggie chuckled as Mike got on her bike and pretended to start racing with her.

"Don't be fooled, ladies and gentlemen." Mike made a microphone out of her closed fist and constricted her throat muscles to make her voice sound electronic.

"There are two fine competitors in our race today. In lane one, wearing blue shorts and a black tank top, is a you-know-what called Thunder B! She looks mean today, folks, and more than ready to take on her competition. In lane two, wearing a black leotard and exposing her ... I mean showing off her talents, is you-know-who calling herself Furious F.

33

Ah, yes. She's batting her eyelashes at Thunder B trying to disrupt her concentration."

Mike got herself into a ready position and gritted her teeth at Maggie. Maggie could only laugh, sometimes throwing back her head in melodrama, sometimes shyly covering her mouth like a child.

"And they're ready," Mike's announcer voice continued. "But, what's this? Furious F has already worked up a sweat and she's ... she's wiping sweat from her ... her chest! It's working, folks. Furious F has Thunder B flustered. She's starting to wobble. Her bike is shaking now! It's bucking and, oh, no! Ladies and gentlemen, it's a sad day for B's everywhere. Thunder B is out of the race. She took quite a fall. The F's of the world now have control."

Mike lowered her head as she walked away from the bikes in pretend defeat. Straight people around her were laughing and some were clapping as she waved to them with a slight smile.

"Well, don't leave me here," Maggie protested. "If I won I should at least be helped off this thing!"

Mike looked back, stuck her hands in the waistband of her shorts, and then shrugged her shoulders as if powerless to help. Two other women who certainly looked like they might be butches rushed to Maggie's aid.

Maggie quickly draped a towel around her shoulders and only half smiled as her eyes searched the room. "How embarrassing."

"You loved it," Mike said.

"Okay, so it was fun, but I have to find Sheila ... She should be on the treadmill, but I don't see her."

Mike couldn't see over as many people as Maggie could, but she tried her best to locate the tall woman she assumed to be Sheila. She laughed a little to herself as she realized the scene she had just caused, but she knew Maggie was a performer and all performers loved attention. The banter between them was natural and relaxed, and Mike began to feel a little younger, a little more alive.

"I can't seem to..."

"Do you always do that?" Mike asked.

"What?"

34

"Stop in the middle of sentences and pause between every three words?"

"Oh. I don't ... know."

"See? You just did it again."

"Did what?" a voice behind Mike asked.

"There you are! I've been looking all over for you."

"Did what?" Sheila asked again.

"Oh, Sheila, this is Mike. She says I pause every three words and don't finish my..."

"Sentences? You're right, Mike," Sheila said. "She always does that."

Mike stuck out her chest victoriously but winced when Sheila grabbed her shoulder.

"You're not supposed to know that about her," Sheila teased. "I'm the only one who knows her that well."

Mike felt the almost brute strength in Sheila's hand and it almost scared her, but when she was scared, she immediately fought back.

"I notice things quickly," she said jerking away from Sheila's grip.

"Just kidding, Mike. Just kidding."

Maggie intervened immediately. "Sheila's just scary because she's strong. She wouldn't hurt a fly. Let's go to the pool."

"I'm not finished with my workout yet," Mike said, eyeing Sheila's grin.

"Well, I have to go," Maggie said. "I need to be wet."

Mike and Sheila continued to glare at each other until Mike backed off in respect for Sheila's territory. Sheila had to defend her position and protect her relationship. Mike was the intruder, and she knew she had no right to act too friendly.

Mike took her time on each body machine to be certain Maggie and Sheila were gone. She didn't bother with the pool, just sponge-bathed away from the open shower stalls and dressed for home. She was surprised to find them sitting in the lobby.

"Finally," Maggie said. "We thought you had shriveled up or gone down the drain. Sheila made up all these wonderful stories about what might have happened to you. So funny.

Would you like to come over for coffee or something?"

"Maybe meet the cats?" Sheila added.

"I don't know," Mike said. "It's kinda late."

"You're coming," Maggie said as she stood to leave. "We didn't wait here an hour so you could tell us what time it is. Follow us in your car. We're near the river."

With that they quickly left. Mike had no choice but to follow.

❏ ❏

Mike waited in the hallway of the big house while Maggie and Sheila scurried around finding cats and checking mail. They acted married: full of routine and familiarities and not quite sure whose guest Mike was supposed to be.

"You're allowed to come in, you know," Sheila finally said. Mike nodded as she tried to decide which person she should follow.

"We'll be in here," Maggie shouted. "Make sure your shoes are clean and come into the living room."

"Wherever that is," Mike said under her breath. She inched past an old piano and carefully stepped over a pile of stuffed animals that seemed out of place in the middle of the floor. The house was dark, the kind of house that would never allow sunlight. It reminded her of the haunted mansion at Disneyland.

"Don't mind the stuff on the floor," Maggie shouted again. "Sheila's into crafts and she makes critters."

Mike tried to see exactly what kind of critters she was stepping over, but the darkness made them only shadows. She looked around her at overfilled bookcases, leather bracelets, and what seemed to be a real cat sitting on a banister.

"That's Broom Hilda," Sheila said from behind her. "She guards the stairway. Mag's in here. Coffee, soda, beer, or what?"

"Soda, I guess," Mike said.

"The beer's colder."

"I don't really drink."

"Hey, Mag?" Sheila said, heading for the kitchen. "We actually know a dyke who doesn't drink."

36

Mike finally found Maggie stretched out on pillows in front of the fireplace. She looked around in vain for an empty chair.

"Right down here," Maggie said. "Sheila makes pillows, too. Besides, she'll have a fit if you move any of her stuff off the chairs."

Mike found a reasonably comfortable spot on the floor and unconsciously moved away from Maggie.

"Does Sheila play guitar?" Mike asked, checking out the empty guitar case next to her.

"No, not yet. That belongs to ... me. I just did it again, didn't I?"

Mike nodded nervously.

"It must be from practicing the incantations. We just had a meeting of the coven yesterday."

"Like in witches?"

"Oh yes. I'm a witch. You don't have to look so shocked. A lot of women are witches."

Mike swallowed to make sure her courage was still with her. She didn't believe in witches, so she wasn't afraid, but she wasn't so sure she wanted to be around people who believed they had the power of witches.

"Do witches use leather?" Mike asked, examining a studded leather cuff.

"Not usually. That's a present from one of the dykes in my S&M group. She makes them."

"S&M, huh?"

"You look like you swallowed a cat," Sheila said as she returned with Mike's soda.

"She just found out I'm a witch."

"I'm not," Sheila said. "We're renting a cabin next weekend. Do you wanna come out and do some snow hiking or somethin'?"

"Where is it?" Mike felt herself almost cowering. "I mean, I don't think I can. Besides, I hate the cold weather."

"Then why the hell are you in Buffalo?"

"I don't know," Mike answered thoughtfully. "I came back after the Marine Corps for my father, stayed for a lover, and have to stay till someone else comes back."

"You know, Sheila," Maggie said, "I'm not sure I want to go out there this weekend either. I have all this work to do."

"No problem. Jan and Marge are comin'. They're better in the woods anyway."

"Sheila's such a Girl Scout! I love it out there, but the cold makes my asthma act up and—"

"I said it was okay," Sheila interrupted almost angrily.

Mike watched the face-off for a moment before making a show of checking her watch.

"Oh, gee," she said. "I promised someone I'd call and I'm late." She quickly made her way toward the first door she could find. "Thanks for the soda. This is a nice house. Uh, have a nice weekend, Sheila. Uh, I guess I'll see ya at the spa."

She hesitated to see if either of them was going to show her out. When neither moved, she waved, closed the door, and headed home.

"Finally!" Mike grabbed the airmail letter from her mailbox and raced down the hall to her door. A smiling face was inked across the back flap, a sign from Ana and a way to check for tampering.

My beautiful woman,
Do you know how much I miss you and love you?
Things are so bad here...

Mike read with tears in her eyes, then held the letter close to her heart. She anxiously prayed for help in getting Ana back. Though she wasn't religious, she believed that somewhere a force existed that was on her side, a force that had protected her when she was alone on the streets and guided her when there was too much trouble to run from. She needed that guidance now. Helplessness was worse than lost love.

It's not time for me to come back yet. There are things I have to do, things I must go through. Live your life, my dear woman. Be strong. Be happy. Know how much I love you, no matter what.

Mike checked the envelope for words from Amalia. When she found no note or picture, she decided it was too soon.

38

Time meant different things to children. A day was like a wink and a month more like a day.

❏ ❏

"Mike? Maggie. Sheila's out of town and I thought I'd call and see if you're busy. I'd like to talk to you about a new song."

"I'm just writing letters," Mike said.

"Oh. When you're done?"

"We can talk now."

"Oh. I mean, I want you to come over," Maggie said.

Mike hesitated. It was almost spring, and she had written close to a hundred letters to Ana and Amalia. She told them about the weather, Women's Studies, the computer center, her neighbors, anything that would make them remember home, make them feel they had never left. Each day, she tried to give them more of herself; each day, it got harder.

"I guess I could come for a while," Mike said.

"God, I wish you wouldn't do that."

"Do what?"

"Do you have any idea how sexy your voice is on the phone? When you lower it like that it just ... drives me crazy!"

Mike didn't know how to respond. Something tickled her butch pride. She had been so busy missing Ana that it never occurred to her anyone else would even notice her, and she didn't know if she really wanted the attention.

Without a thought about what reaction it might cause, she lowered her voice again. "I'll be over in twenty minutes."

"Okay," Maggie whispered.

Maggie opened her door with a smile and a whispered "Hello." She didn't move back to let Mike enter, but instead blocked the entrance, as if waiting for a different greeting. Mike lowered her eyes nervously and stuck her hands in her pockets. It wasn't like her to kiss or hug everybody she met. That was for phonies or people who were insecure.

Maggie let her pass and then led her to the couch, the only uncluttered seat in the room.

"Tell me what you think," Maggie said. She cleared her throat, breathed some asthma medicine, and then launched into a funny song about rumors and community and affairs. The punchline was that the only woman who truly knew her

39

was her beautician. Mike laughed, mesmerized by Maggie's voice. Making music was her fantasy, and singers her idols.

"Why don't you sing onstage?" Mike asked. "You could be great!"

"I would have. I wanted to sing at the Met, but my asthma got in the way."

"You sound fine to me," Mike glowed. "Maybe you can't be a soloist at the Met, but judging from all those parties I've seen you perform at, you sure can draw a crowd."

Maggie looked at her with puppy-dog eyes and played with her fingers like a child who wanted something she shouldn't have.

"Do you really think so, Mike?"

"I know so! Can you sing some others?"

"Kiss me," Maggie said softly.

Mike was about to laugh when she realized that Maggie wasn't joking. She knew she shouldn't, and she knew kisses in the lesbian community often meant more than they were sometimes supposed to, but she was drawn to Maggie's need.

Carefully she put an arm around Maggie's neck so her head could rest on Mike's elbow. Carefully she leaned toward her, and softly she kissed her. Mike felt an urgency in Maggie's kiss and she wanted to pull away quickly, before it was too late; but she couldn't deny that Maggie knew how to kiss, nor could she negate the need in herself to feel another woman's passion or desire.

When they finally pulled apart, they couldn't meet each other's eyes. Mike still felt like she was cheating on Leslie. Now that was compounded by the feeling she was cheating on Ana. Then there was Sheila to consider.

"Sheila and I don't make love anymore," Maggie said to her lap. "We've talked and talked. We're just about ready to see other people."

"You're breaking up?"

"No. We're just ... it's just okay."

Mike shifted further away from Maggie. Things always seemed to happen so quickly in the gay community. No one dated or flirted or built friendships. It seemed everyone wanted some kind of commitment immediately, or at least a sign that commitment was just around the corner.

To break the tension, Mike opened her mouth wide, yawned, and then bared her teeth like a cat.

"Hair balls," she said.

Maggie looked at her in amazement. "What?"

"Hair balls!" Mike repeated her catlike yawn, and with their shared laughter they both knew they had started something that would forever bond them.

MISSING

Mike, Maggie, and Sheila became a strange threesome during the early spring. They went to the spa almost every day, and listened to music and laughed together almost every night. Maggie paid special attention to Sheila. Mike tried her best to become Sheila's friend. The snow continued through March, and the letters from Ana became more and more desperate.

> My beautiful woman,
> There is so much I can't write, so much I am not able to say. You have to come here, not only to help me, but also to see this country that tears me apart. There is so much beauty, so much despair. When can you come? Amalia talks about you all the time. She calls you her computer and when she climbs on me and plays she says I am your replacement. Come for her birthday in June. Come for me. Let me love you here.

❏ ❏

Mike visited Emma, the local feminist bookstore, to search for more stories of Chile. The volunteers were always helpful,

42

especially a woman named Jackie who Mike thought was beautiful. Mike needed smiles and kindness. She needed warmth. She needed the strength of her history to make the right decisions for Ana and Amalia.

She asked for an extended vacation from work but was told she could only have ten days. It was six thousand miles to Santiago, and she needed extra time off in case of an emergency. She'd have to find a way to get more than ten days' vacation without losing her job. Money was her next problem. She was paying the rent on Ana's apartment so she'd have a place to live when she returned. She'd also sent money to Amalia, bought presents for friends, even purchased a used car for Leslie, because people thought she owed her it to her. Overtime pay was her only resort.

She took on the work of three people, slaving more than twelve hours a day installing computer terminals. Often, she collapsed on her apartment floor, with her beeper still on her belt.

My beautiful woman,
    Why have your letters stopped? There were once many, so much love. I worry now. I love you and need you. Are you coming?

Dear Computer,
    I miss you very much. You are the only one who writes to me. I have new monkey bars named Ana. I love you. Amalia.

Dear woman,
    Your letters are not the same. Your voice is different on the phone. What are you keeping from me? You must keep your strength. I love you and need you. When I draw, I draw your face. When I dream, I dream of you. There is so much I need to go through, so much struggle. I want you to be here when I do, to hold me, comfort me, share it with me. Give me your strength. Please come soon.

43

Dear Ana, my beautiful Latin American woman,

I am trying everything to get you back and am working to be with you as soon as I can. I have to get you a special visa and I may be able to pull strings at the university. I miss you. I need to know you're truly there. I'm coming in June. Please be there smiling. All my love.

❏ ❏

Mike sat on Maggie's porch, her face turned toward the warm May sun. Together, they harmonized to the Everly Brothers.

"I pick up my passport tomorrow," Mike said when they finished singing. "I need to leave information with you. In case I don't make it back."

"You're ... going to come back ... aren't you?"

"I can only try, Mag. You never know in Chile. If I'm not back by the last Sunday in June, you have to contact the State Department and tell them I can't get out. I'll leave you all my papers, my birth certificate, identification, travel itinerary. The people at the State Department are the only ones who'll be able to get me out if anything happens."

"But, Mike. I think I—"

"Oh," Mike interrupted, "I told my boss I'm having a D&C done in Fredonia. I need you to call and pretend you're my sister. Tell him there's been some complications and I'll be out for a couple of weeks. They won't know where to call, so I'm safe."

"But, Mike?"

"I have to go, Mag. I'm going to Fredonia to say good-bye to a few people, just in case. I'll see you before I leave for the airport."

She gently kissed Maggie's hand, then made a mental note to send her a single red rose so she wouldn't forget her.

My dear woman,

I can't believe it! I'll see you in two weeks and I want it so badly. I'm scared, too. I think of you walking by my side down the streets of my childhood. I think of you sharing the dinner table at my house. I think of you looking at me, touching me, feeling me. I

44

think of you and me loving each other and, oh, God, I can't stand it.. You are doing more than just coming here. You are bridging time, space, and history all together. All these months we have been apart have changed only the expression of our feelings, but they are there, strong as ever.

One last warning is that we are not free here. I can't offer you the paradise I would like to offer you. And it is cold, very cold. The opposite season of Buffalo, but come! Come soon or I will die of anxiety!

❏ ❏

Mike drove to the insurance company in Fredonia where Sharon worked. At first, Sharon didn't recognize her. Mike's hair was shorter than ever, and the workouts at the spa had made her leaner, almost masculine.

"I need some life insurance," Mike said.

"Aren't there any insurance agents in Buffalo?" Sharon's smile and voice were as soft as Mike remembered them. She couldn't help feeling the same tenderness, the same warmth, the love she had harbored now for sixteen years.

"I wanted you to get the business," Mike answered. They were so at ease with each other that, for a moment, Mike forgot about Ana, her fear of Chile, all the plans she and Ana were making. Their hands touched for an electrifying second when Mike signed the application. In that instant, Mike knew that the promise she had made so long ago, the promise to never not love Sharon, was the most real promise she had ever made. A butch's first love was for always, no matter what.

"I'll need the first month's premium and some medical information," Sharon said.

"You married yet?" Mike wrote the check before cautiously checking Sharon's eyes.

"No. I'm working on it, though. Are you?"

Mike shook her head.

"You're not? I thought I was the only single thirty-year-old left."

"I'm working on it," Mike teased. "Maybe I'll beat you to it."

"I've been engaged to a guy for six years now," Sharon said. "He's just not ready yet."

Mike wanted to tell her it would never work out, that the guy would have married her by now if he really loved her, but to protect Sharon's feelings, she kept her peace. She'd find out someday. Besides, Mike couldn't do anything about it.

She didn't know how to say good-bye without exposing her feelings, so she shook Sharon's hand in a businesslike manner and waved to everyone else in the office.

She decided to walk to Maple Avenue so she could enjoy the tall trees and the gentle breezes from the lake. Winters were hell, but God, she loved her hometown in the summer. She wished Ana and Amalia were with her so they could see her school, her street, the trees she adored climbing. She wanted to share memories of her youth, a youth fading much too soon.

She also wanted to see her parents, but somehow she felt they had already said their good-byes a long time ago. Instead, she strolled up and down the street she had once owned and sat on the curb facing the tree that bore her initials. A burst of wind made her jump to her feet. In a race against age, lost love, and the secrets of childhood that sustain innocence, she ran across the street and into the yard that held her tree.

With no fear of failure, no thought of danger, she climbed. It was easy. The tree cradled her as if she were a child returning to her mother's lap and soon, almost too soon, she was near the top. Standing on the strongest branch, she sucked in the wind that seemed to cheer her, then settled in to rest in the tree's leafy lap. From her roost, she could just see the front door of her parents' house. It was from here that she gathered her strength and waved good-bye.

❏ ❏

LAN Chile Airlines left JFK Airport right on schedule. As far as Mike could tell, she was the only non-Spanish-speaking person on board. She tried to remember some of the words she had learned from Ana, but it had been too long. The stewardess began asking everyone what they wanted to drink. Mike felt embarrassed. She pretended to cough while

46

pointing toward a coffeepot. When the stewardess poured the coffee, Mike automatically said, "Thank you."

"You're welcome," the stewardess answered in English.

She nodded at the stewardess with a smile and took a deep breath to try and relax. Fourteen hours was a long time to be up in the air, but thoughts and dreams of what was to come kept her busy.

By the time the plane was over Cuba, it was 3 a.m. Others were sleeping, but Mike stayed wide-eyed as she watched lightning strike the Cuban waters. She thought of her teaching days at Women's Studies, about Communism and Marxism and doing "Dyke for a Day." How could anyone be a dyke for only a day? She laughed as she remembered the many times she had sat in a circle of very young women and told her life story. They'd listen so innocently and ask questions about everything from sex to silicones. For some it was the only day they actually knew they were talking to a dyke.

Good old Women's Studies. Mike was a feminist, but not the kind scholars quoted. She lived their theories and the oppression they studied. She couldn't choose to look different. She couldn't choose a career that demanded femininity. She couldn't talk about whether or not to come out as a lesbian; she'd been out since the day she was born.

She remembered her church choir. She loved to sing, and in Fredonia, the choir was just about the only chance someone had to show off her ability; but Mike had been born too soon. The priest said she was a girl and had to wear a hat. He said she couldn't wear pants under her robe even if no one could see. She had argued that men didn't have to wear hats, so neither would she. He argued back that because women were lowlier, they had to cover their heads. When she'd told him he was full of shit, he'd told her she couldn't sing.

She had been kicked out of Girl Scouts for refusing to wear gloves. She had also thought it was silly to learn to sew when the boys were learning how to survive.

In high school, she'd decorated the gym for her prom, only to watch her favorite girl dance with someone else.

The storm continued as the plane crossed over Bolivia. La Paz, a ten-minute layover, was Mike's first taste of a different reality. People were herded off the plane onto an open field. Broken warplanes and tank parts from local unrest littered the short tarmac and the path to the tiny terminal. Bolivian police watched their every step. They instilled such fear in Mike that she had to go to the bathroom. She didn't know how to ask where it was, and each time she tried to approach a policeman, he looked at her steely-eyed and scared her more. She was trying to be tough, but this was obviously not her turf. When she finally could hold it no more, she grabbed her crotch like a man might and jerked her head in a questioning gesture. The policeman immediately acknowledged her and practically led her to the men's room. Luckily, it was almost empty. She swaggered into a stall as if she belonged and did what she had to do.

Children begged everyone for pesos and Mike shuddered as she followed everyone else's lead and shooed them away. As the passengers returned to the plane, Mike thought she saw a llama on the runway, but she wasn't sure. Of this she was certain: La Paz was not New York. She was a long way from home.

The plane took off on its final leg to Santiago. Clouds blocked the sunrise, but Mike still marveled at the beauty of the Andes. She knew where she was now. She had listened enough, studied enough, felt enough of Chile's history to know exactly where she was. She caught herself searching the Andes for signs of hidden peasants or rebels. All she saw were mountain curves, gentle swirls, and peaks pointing reverently toward the ocean. She wanted to remember every inch, every color and tone. She knew Ana would ask. She wouldn't disappoint her.

Soon, she would see them. She was sure the sound of her heartbeat matched the engine's roar as the plane touched down in Ana's land. Every part of her was rushing from the plane before it even stopped. Only the whiteness of her knuckles as she gripped the seat told her she was still inside the plane. "Be cool," she told herself. "There's junta here. Be cool."

The glassed terminal was deadly silent as herded passengers presented their passports and awaited permission to leave with their luggage. Mike didn't know which way to look. Desperately, she pretended she had done this before. Defiantly she presented her visitor's visa and waited for the cold official to nod his okay. Only after he returned her passport did she see the faces beyond the glass. Ana's and Amalia's smiles broke the terror. A white-haired man with a moustache waved from behind them. Mike knew it was Ana's father.

"Ola! Ola!"

Mike rushed to throw her arms around Ana. She needed so badly to feel her warmth, to know she was real.

"How was your trip?" Ana gave Mike a short hug and then quickly pushed her away. "This is my father, Fernando."

He presented his hand gallantly and with a special class that Mike hadn't known was in Ana's blood.

"Amalia?" Ana pulled Amalia closer. "Your computer is here!"

Mike knelt to give Amalia a hug, but she, too, stood back and only smiled her greeting. Mike's heart felt crushed beneath her. The excitement, the anticipation vanished in a ripping second and the cold Chilean winter whistled through her soul. She tried to gather her poise and act like the guest they were all expecting.

"And your mother?" she asked.

"She's at home. Waiting for us, for you!"

Ana was still bubbling. Her smile brought out all the parts of her Mike loved, and Mike recognized the shimmering twinkle in her eyes. She had been warned. She would wait until they were alone to give her love. Though Mike felt no inhibitions, she realized Ana was with a parent. It didn't matter that she was thirty-five and had a child of her own, she was still her father's daughter. Gay oppression was no different in either America.

"Tonight, my brother and sister will come for tea and to meet you," Ana said. "Tomorrow, my father will take us on a car trip, and tomorrow night, you will meet my friend Lola. Next weekend, the whole family will go to the beach, and Monday, I will take you to the university."

Mike nodded and tried to shake the cobwebs from her head. She had never dreamed of being treated like a special family guest. She had come to be with her lover and a special little girl. She'd do what she had to, what Ana wanted, but she didn't need tours or politics or other acquaintances; she needed Ana.

❑ ❑

Ana's family toasted, patted, bowed to, and smiled at Mike throughout the day. Ana and Amalia interpreted and the entire family seemed to accept Mike as a special person in Ana's life, someone who cared enough about their country to come and visit.

Finally, it was time for Ana to show Mike where she would sleep. Gratefully, Mike ascended the stairs in the old wooden house. This would be their time alone. Amalia was snuggled in across the hall and all was quiet. Heating oil was scarce and expensive, so the nights were spent bundled and almost breathless.

Carefully Mike pulled Ana toward her. For a chilling moment, they laid their heads on each other's shoulder. Mike could feel Ana's need, her desire, but when she tried to kiss her ever so gently, Ana again pulled away.

"My parents are below us. I can't do this here."

"We'll be quiet," Mike pleaded. "They'll never know."

Again she tried to pull Ana near; again, Ana pulled away. "I can't. I can't do this."

Mike lay back on her bed and pulled the blankets up to warm her. She felt like a child, the cold child she once was. She saw the cemetery in Fredonia flash before her, and the vision of herself huddled on the ground near the headstones chilled her even more. She was alone. She had traveled six thousand miles to be completely, utterly, alone.

She rolled toward the wall, tugging the blankets over her head. She didn't want to see Ana now. She hadn't wanted sex, only a loving touch, a warming hug, a soft awareness of her caring. Even a friend would have given that.

When morning came, it was Amalia who broke the silence.

"Hi, Mike, get up! We're goin' on a car trip and my gramma has breakfast ready."

Amalia's dimples were back. They gave Mike courage to face the day. In the distant morning, she heard the clanging of cans.

"The curfew is over," Amalia explained. "They're selling heating oil on the street. Did you know you have to take a cold shower?"

Mike shuddered at the thought. Suddenly, Amalia threw herself on Mike's bed and hugged her quickly.

"I'm glad you're here, Mike."

She was down the stairs in a flash. Immediately, the house came alive. Doorbells rang, pots and pans crashed, someone whistled a strange tune. Through it all, Ana barely spoke.

"Can I hug you good morning?" Mike asked.

Ana came to her in her nightgown. They spent a wonderful minute in each other's arms, but only a minute. Ana's thoughts were on Mike's appearance, how she would look to other Chileans and to her family. She searched through Mike's suitcase for something suitable, but found nothing that didn't seem too male, too working class, too gay.

Mike tried to reassure her. "Don't worry. People usually like me for who I am, not how I dress."

"They'll know you are a bootch," Ana said angrily. Mike knew her concern was real.

"It's butch, not bootch. No puckers, see? Not bootch, just butch."

Mike's eyes softened. She wanted Ana to know she understood her worries, but she also wanted Ana to know she was proud of who she was. No amount of oppression was going to change that.

They settled on a sweater and black slacks. Ana said they'd find a place on the road that sold ponchos, so Mike wouldn't stand out as much.

Amalia sat between Ana and Mike in the backseat of the ten-year-old Mercedes and busied herself playing with a computer game Mike had bought her.

"Mercedes are not so expensive here." Fernando struggled with English, but Mike thought he managed well, at least better than she did in Spanish. "Not like in America. Now, it's time for you to see Chile," he said with obvious pride.

Mike readied her camera, but she wasn't prepared for what she saw. As they drove down a main street that followed the Mapocho River, Ana pointed out bloodstains on the cement banks and told of the countless bodies found floating there during the coup. The city was like New York or Toronto, only twenty years behind. Gucci shoe stores and Coca-Cola signs lined the otherwise dismal streets. The people walked with their eyes to the ground. To Ana, this was their main sign of defeat and desolation.

"Always, they walked proudly," she said. "But now, now they have no hope."

Overcrowded buses and taxis with signs saying, "Be Careful" sped by them as they made their way to the city's outskirts.

"The houses on the left were built by Allende's people, for the workers and the peasants." Ana waited until Mike could get a good look. "They're not bad. Like good housing projects in America. The huts on the right were once the homes of the workers and peasants."

Mike looked sadly at the structures people called home.

"But the soldiers moved into the good housing during the coup," said Ana. "Now, the peasants and workers are back in the shacks."

Mike could feel Ana's pain. She wanted so badly to take her hand and comfort her. The most she could do was to move her foot over the hump in the middle of the floor and try to feel closer to Ana's body.

They continued their journey into the countryside, past signs that said cameras were forbidden and past ragged children on horseback who wanted to smile for pictures. They stopped at a roadside market where Fernando bartered with the owner so Mike could get a good wool poncho at a decent price.

"You're looking more Chilean now," Ana said proudly as Fernando patted Mike's back.

They drove farther into the hills that led to the mountains and stopped for fresh stone-baked bread. Feeling more comfortable out of the city, Mike decided to walk through the dirt streets by herself. She stopped at the edge of town, atop a small hill looking down on green brick buildings. She felt a familiarity with the way they were built and the layout, and she automatically clenched her fists. Her hair curled in the

52

misty wind and she could smell the salt from the ocean.

Ana came up beside her. "The barracks of the junta's army. This is where they train to kill."

"It looks like Camp Pendleton. Where I was stationed in the Marines."

Ana nodded and motioned for Mike to return to the car.

As Ana walked away, Mike called her name. When she turned, Mike snapped her picture against the background of broken houses crowding each other on muddy hills.

"We must return before the curfew," said Fernando. "We'll stop to buy meat for tomorrow's lunch." He winked at Ana to let her know the occasion was special enough to bear the expense.

Amalia put her head in Mike's lap, stretched her feet across Ana's legs, and played with Mike's earlobe. Her giggles erased the pictures in Mike's mind, and her body formed a bridge to Ana that Mike wished she could cross.

The car slowed as they neared the edge of the city. Ana and Amalia instinctively sat at attention.

"Put the camera under your poncho," Ana whispered without looking at Mike. "Quickly! Say nothing and don't smile."

The roadblock was swarming with armed soldiers. Mike's neck itched as her nervous sweat mixed with new wool. Fernando stopped the car and immediately reached for his identification. A guard said something in Spanish and Fernando quickly got out of the car. He disappeared inside a guard shack as everyone in the car sat perfectly still.

A metallic tap made Mike jump. Ana swiftly leaned over to roll down the window. A soldier's rifle inched through the gap to prod Mike's shoulder.

"*Donde vas?*"

"He wants to know where you're going. Tell him!"

"Santiago."

"*Americana?*" He prodded harder with his gun.

"*Si.*"

"Show him your passport, carefully."

As Mike reached beneath her poncho for her papers, her camera slid from her lap. She knew the man could see it. He gathered his English and told her to step out of the car.

"No camera," he said. "No camera."

He motioned for Mike to give it to him and she did so with a slight smile.

"*Americana, heh? Communista? Eh? Communista de America?*"

Mike shook her head submissively. "It's empty," she said. "No film."

He jerked it from her hand and checked it while another man guarded her. Satisfied that it was empty, he tossed it back at her.

"No pictures," he said again sternly and pointed her back to the car.

It took several more minutes for Fernando to return. When he did, they drove off slowly and said nothing until they were far away from the danger.

"My father says they warned him about a broken headlight," Ana said. "They told him he must get it fixed and then checked his papers again and again."

Mike knew that wasn't the real reason they'd detained him. She slid her still-clenched hand into her pocket and opened it to release the roll of film that held Ana's picture.

❏ ❏

Ana and Mike spent the night talking from opposite sides of the tiny bedroom. Though she still allowed no physical contact, Ana was warmer. Mike was grateful for that. They never again spoke of the roadblock or the film. Mike thought they made a good team. She only wished Ana felt the same.

❏ ❏

The country of Chile is only one hundred miles wide, so the trip to the beach was not a long one. Mike was surprised at the elegance of the beach house, the richness it possessed in a land so battered and seemingly poor. The beach was also different than she had imagined: not California-crowded or Florida-white, but rather a tapestry of color and contours, vegetation and life.

From the windows of the cottage, she could see a sandy hill covered with paths that led to jagged rocks along the coastline. As the others did family things and readied the house for the weekend, Mike grabbed a large branch to use as a walking stick and ventured to the water. She hoped Ana would eventually sneak away and join her, but the lure of the ocean was stronger than her need for companionship.

She followed the most worn path until she reached the crest of the hill. To the south, dunes and patches of weeds led to rocky slopes that climbed to smooth, red rock ledges that jutted into the sea. To the north, cactus-bordered paths meandered up grassy hills that seemed to float above the mist. Either direction seemed an adventure worth trying. She chose the hills to improve her view.

She climbed one hill after another, checking often for Ana or any sign from the cottage and constantly stopping to absorb the beauty that surrounded her. Suddenly she heard voices from a hill beyond her, male voices shouting at each other in Spanish. She gathered her poncho around her and squatted behind a cactus. She knew the green and brown of her garment would blend with the colors around her. While keeping a firm hold on her walking stick, she bowed her head to conceal herself more. She listened to the voices, to guage their direction and distance.

"It's a goat! Mike, get up! They're chasing a wild goat!"

Ana rushed up the hills waving her arms and laughing. Mike looked toward the sky in embarrassment. She had been ready to fight, to kill. She had almost wet her pants.

Ana finally reached her and couldn't control her laughter. "You have to learn Spanish." She laughed again and tried to catch her breath. "They are yelling to each other about a wild goat. It's on one of the hills. It butted one of the men and they're chasing it. Come! We'll help them find it!"

She pulled Mike's poncho and led her in a full run.

"You were watching me," Mike said. "From the house. From the window."

"Of course! You think your Latin American woman would leave you out here all by yourself?"

Mike's heart pounded. For the first time in almost three days, she and Ana smiled warmly at each other.

"Come on," Ana pleaded. "It'll get away."

Mike ran after her as well as she could. The poncho was like a dress, and she wasn't used to her legs being hindered.

"What does a wild goat look like?" she asked when they stopped to scan the hills below them.

"Like a goat. You know. Only a wild goat."

"Don't Chilean goats look different than American goats?" Ana laughed again as she led the way to another hill.

"Wait! I think I see it!" Mike pointed with her stick. "See, over there, going toward the ocean! And look, there's more!"

Ana searched the coastline in the direction Mike was pointing. "Mike. I have to give you a new lesson," she said very seriously, as she knelt in the grass to rest. "The animals you're pointing at are llamas, not goats."

Mike squinted, then felt herself turning red. She pretended to be angry as she threw her stick to the ground and sat beside Ana.

"What the hell are llamas doing on a beach? And goats? You just let them run wild here, or what?"

"Over there is an ostrich," Ana answered softly. "All things should be free. This is where they live."

Together, they watched the waves and the llamas. Mike wanted to hold her as they listened to the power of the sea, to share its strength with her, to feel its pounding rhythm between them, but still they couldn't touch.

"Don't worry," Ana said knowingly. "I feel it, too."

❏ ❏

At dusk, hundreds of people flocked to the beach. They lined the rocks, dangling their feet over every jagged edge. From a distance, they were like seagulls waiting for the last ship to come into port. Mike and Ana found a spot, and Amalia chose a seat on Mike's lap. Slowly, the sky began its symphony. Vibrant pink swelled to meet a gentle purple, forming an eyelid that would soon meet with the sea. The sun turned orange, then red, then the brightest gold as it gave its last wink to the day. The pink remained, a reminder of the copper mines, while strong clouds joined together in gripping strength. All the people looked up as the pink finally faded away, and then the strange array of spectators scattered in the darkness to await another day.

Ana carefully took Mike's hand, concealed by the poncho, as the waves crashed against the rocks below. Amalia snuggled closer to share the moment, and the three became almost one in their separate vigils. On a distant hill Mike eyed red-tipped cigarettes of two silhouettes who appeared to be men. Their faces were only slightly illuminated as they puffed and talked, but Mike could see they were dressed differently than the others who had come to the beach. Almost simultaneously, she and Ana took Amalia's hands and playfully jumped to their feet. They didn't look back as they sang their way to the beach house.

❑ ❑

With only one day left before Mike's departure, Ana decided to take Mike to the port city of Valparaiso.

"I think you'll love it there," Ana said. "The houses are full of color and they sit nestled in the hills that lead to the water. The fishermen's boats are also all colors and sizes. We'll eat lunch by the water and be back before Amalia gets out of school."

The thought of spending time alone with Ana, even if it was on a bus or at lunch in a strange place, made Mike want to look and act her best. She survived an extra minute in the cold shower and sang Latin songs as she shivered herself dry. It was true that she and Ana had grown closer, but it was a spiritual, mental, and political closeness. Mike also needed the physical to sustain her. She couldn't wait to sit close to Ana on the bus or sneak a touch on a walk. She wore tight but comfortable jeans and a black shirt covered by a Chilean wool sweater. Her hair refused to be anything but curly, but her hands were warm, and the pride of being with the woman she loved made her look taller and stronger.

"We have to pick up Lola. She wants to come with us."

The warmth left Mike's hands. Though she tried to be friendly to Lola and not expose her feelings, she couldn't smile. She sat near a stranger on the bus and glared at Ana as she and Lola talked and laughed. Lola's lipstick was too red, her eyes, too painted. Mike knew she was a good person, but her influence on Ana was too great. By the time they reached the water, Ana also had red lips and painted eyes. They were ready to use the power of their made-up womanhood to seduce any man who looked at them. It was the only power no one could take away.

They walked to the end of a short pier and entered a restaurant that gave them a full view of the water. Winter was closer now that it was almost July, and a heavy fog crept across the waves. Mike allowed Ana and Lola to walk ahead of her. As she fell into step behind them, a man jumped from the shadows and took her picture. Her first impulse was to put up her hands in self-defense, but Ana quickly pushed her arms down and grabbed her poncho. After they had been seated for a few minutes, the same man approached their table and presented the photograph to Mike.

"Free of charge. For the American tourist."

Ana and Lola exchanged knowing glances before proceeding to order a fish concoction that Mike would never eat. They giggled and pointed at boats that could be seen through the grayness.

"Don't look around," Ana warned as she continued pointing toward the water. "The men in suits are outside, by the red-and-white boat. They're watching us. Be happy. Be excited about the boats."

Mike did as she was told and then quickly pulled out her camera. After Ana nodded that pictures were okay here, Mike took a dozen. Eventually, she put the camera back on the table, pointed it toward the men on the pier, and set the automatic timer. One minute later, it snapped a clear photograph that Mike would carry with her to Buffalo.

Mike spent the last night of her visit with Ana's family and then alone with Amalia and Ana. They spoke of the Buffalo summer, possibilities for jobs, plans to get out of Chile, things Mike should take with her as a messenger, and every detail about every person they could think of.

"I'll get you back by Christmas, squirt."

Amalia gave her one of her big squeezes and left for bed with tears in her eyes. Ana and Mike had nothing more to say. The trip had been great but awful. The tension was too much but unavoidable. Mike was glad she had come, but wished she hadn't. Not once did either speak of feelings for the other or plans for a future together.

Amalia didn't want to say good-bye again and so left for school before Mike got up. Ana and her parents escorted Mike to the airport in silence.

"You are not on our computer, señor. I am sorry. I have no reservation for you, nothing here that says you arrived from America."

"I'm not a señor," Mike said. "I have my visa and passport right here, and here's a copy of my ticket. Today at 11:30. It says so right here."

"I'm sorry. You are not on my computer."

Mike's patience was thin. She slammed her hand on the counter. "What the hell does that mean?"

Ana interceded quickly and spoke only in Spanish. Mike didn't like the look on her face when she had finished with the clerk.

"They say you don't exist. You never arrived, so you can't leave."

"I'll just make new reservations."

"You can't make new reservations if you're not on their computer. You are not here."

"Well, how the hell can I not be here? What the hell am I supposed to do now?"

Ana looked at her parents with a fear Mike didn't know she was supposed to have.

"Bullshit!" Mike yelled. "Don't look at each other that way! I'll figure out how to get out of here if it kills me!"

She led the way back to the car and they made the hour drive back home. The Spanish flew throughout the car and Mike understood only one or two words.

"Tell them not to talk so fast so I can understand a little," she pleaded, but the rapid Spanish continued. Mike withdrew to solve her problem the best way she knew. She used the same technique as a child when she was cold or hungry or lost or scared. She put herself into a movie and, of course, she was the star. As she visualized her situation, she calculated what a director might say and what the writer intended. She replayed her entire trip in her mind, searching for the hidden clue, the only way out. Then she went to sleep and let her subconscious take over.

59

"We'll call the airport tonight and ask the full name of the supervisor on duty tomorrow. People here hardly ever use a full name unless it's official, right?"

Ana nodded.

"Then we'll call that supervisor and ask for him by name. I'll tell him I'm from the American embassy and have been instructed to call him, that he's the only one who can get me out."

"We'll see." Ana was unsure, but she always trusted Mike's third eye. "I'll call so my Spanish will be understood."

"Everyone's expecting me back on today's plane. I'd better call Buffalo so they don't panic."

The next morning, Señor Gabriel Jorge Cortez put Mike on a 747 with eleven other people bound for Sao Paulo, Brazil. Mike was gone and safe, on her way back to a country that would forever look different. Her relationship with Ana had been tested, but Mike didn't know if it had passed. She cried as the plane flew over Cuba. When they entered American airspace, the stewardess sprayed the cabin with disinfectant and insecticide. Mike turned green, threw up, and didn't remember anything until she landed in New York. Her luggage, of course, was lost. But everything she promised to carry, everything that really counted, was on her. She passed through customs easily, as she was the only American entering, and headed for the plane that would take her back to warmth, friendship, and a feeling of power she had missed.

THE BAND

It took almost two weeks for Mike's luggage to arrive. It had been rerouted through Canada and Oregon, or so she was told, and everything in the suitcases had been rearranged. Ana's letters took longer to be delivered. Many envelopes arrived empty or torn.

> My beautiful woman,
>   You're gone. I watched you fly away and my heart pounded and cried for you. But you are with me, all around me. Everything I do or see, I do and see with you. You are everywhere. I start to draw and it is a picture of you. Amalia plays your tapes, your games, and tells your stories. It's almost time for us to come back. Do what you can. I love you, miss you.

❏ ❏

Mike read the letters differently now. She wasn't sure of Ana's love, though a part of her felt that the love they shared was deeper and greater than any other. They knew each other, felt each other without touching. They could communicate without talking and talk of things no one else could understand, but Mike wanted more than that. She loved women and loved loving them. She was committed to that love as only a butch can be.

Dear Latin American Woman,

I hear so many messages from you. Why did you wait until I was far away to tell me again that you love me? I ached for you, cried for you, even prayed that we could share our love. I'll do everything I can to get you back. I promise. And I'll always love you.

❑ ❑

"Bill? Mike Landetti. Ana's friend." Mike hated making the call, but Ana needed money and Mike needed contacts for jobs so Ana could get a visa. "Ana needs some help and you're the first person on my list."

"She needs help? What kind of help?"

"Money. Anything you can spare. A job, even a cooked-up one to get things rolling."

"No. No. I don't have any time. Tell her I said hello."

Mike checked Bill's name off her list, then crumpled the paper to throw it away. There were friends she knew she could call to get Ana's money, but the visa problem was one she'd have to solve herself. She had tried everyone, all the people who acted so special in Ana's life. Some did what they could, many didn't understand what was needed, and several, including Bill, never even wanted to discuss it. Mike didn't push. Though she needed every bit of help she could get, she also wanted to preserve Ana's dignity and self-respect.

Dear Mike,

Why don't I hear from you? What is happening with my return? When I came home from Lola's a few days after you left, there was a woman standing guard outside my house. She acted like she didn't notice me so I didn't think too much about it. When I went inside it was dark, and there were dogs outside the window. We found the phone and electric lines cut. If you are a foreigner, you are a Communist, that's the way the military thinks.

I need to know if all is okay. I love you, but I feel crazy.

❏ ❏

Mike visited more attorneys and studied international law, but nothing she could come up with was fail-safe. If she did the wrong thing, called the wrong people, or sent the wrong papers into the wrong hands, it would endanger Ana and Amalia. She couldn't risk that. Her feeling of helplessness and isolation grew worse with each day. Finally, she settled on a plan that involved false employment and a request for a visitor's visa. Her fear of making the wrong decision compelled her to hold onto the paperwork for three days before she could even go near a mailbox. Something didn't feel right, and she always tried to trust her Pisces intuition.

She drove for hours, through the city, down the thruway to Fredonia, through the cemetery, and out into the hills. She was trapped. When she got back to Buffalo, she drove to a plaza near her apartment that had an international mailbox. She trembled as she readied the envelope at the slot. Just as she was about to let go, a man walking by flicked a cigarette at her feet. She kept a grip on the envelope as she turned to confront him, but when she recognized the jacket he was wearing, her fears blasted into rage.

"Hey, you! I wanna talk to you!"

Her shouts made him look at her, and she could see he knew what she was after. He started running. Without a thought, she ran after him.

"Come back here, you son of a bitch!"

She chased him through backyards, over fences, across busy streets, and into neighborhoods she had never seen. Her once-crippled legs were on fire beneath her and her heart skipped beats from the lack of oxygen, but she couldn't let him get away. He was fast and much younger. He went through a schoolyard and over another fence, leading Mike far from cars or people. She slowed a little to watch his direction. He backtracked through a schoolyard.

Mike tucked the envelope inside her shirt before stalking him from behind some bushes. She held her breath so he wouldn't hear her panting. She watched him cross the front steps and check behind him. She watched him grow taller as he came nearer to her position. She readied herself, every muscle tensed, all of her military training behind her.

"Gotcha, you shithead!"

Her choke hold was secure. She pulled one of his arms up behind him to hold him still.

"Never mess with a Marine, asshole."

"What do you want, man? I didn't do nothin' to you."

"Where'd you get the jacket?"

"What jacket? I don't know nothin' about a jacket."

Mike jerked the fur collar of the flight jacket. "This jacket, stupid. Kinda heavy on a hot day like this, isn't it?"

"You a cop or somethin'?"

"I might be. I want to know where you got it."

He tried to pull away, but Mike planted her feet and held him. She twisted his arm a little more to make him talk. She feared his size might be too much for her if he was able to turn around.

"I want an answer."

"A friend of mine. A guy I know. He didn't want it anymore, that's all. He gave it to me."

"Your friend a pilot?"

"Yeah. Yeah, that's right. He's a pilot. This here is his jacket."

"How old is this so-called friend?"

"How old? I don't know, man. My age. He's my age."

"Then this is my jacket," Mike said.

"You want the jacket? Take it. Go ahead. I'll give it to you. Free."

"Not yet, shithead." She tightened her grip once more and lowered her voice. "Who gave it to you? What's his name?"

"I don't know. Just some guy I know at a house I go to. Sunset House. A brother's place."

Satisfied that he had told her everything he was going to, she loosened her grip on his arm. "I'm gonna let you go, you hear? I want the jacket back. You take it off nice and easy and I won't go to the cops. Got it?"

"Yeah, yeah. Okay. Just let go. I'll give you your damn jacket."

Mike let go slowly as the man nervously unzipped the jacket. The knife appeared in a flash and ripped through the front of her shirt. She saw blood seep through her sleeve as she instinctively jumped back from the attack. In another instant, he was gone. So was her father's flight jacket. "Son of a bitch! Damn it!"

Part of her wanted to go after him, but he was too far ahead. She unbuttoned her shirt to check the cut. The envelope had blocked the blade; only a superficial scratch marked her chest. The cut on her arm was deeper, but it didn't warrant stitches. She looked lovingly at the torn envelope before tearing it into tiny pieces and throwing it away.

Sunset House was near the expressway, a place Mike had driven by many times. Today she waited at the curb and watched as people came and went. Most of them looked like professionals or artists; many of them were men wearing Moslem garments and carrying books. When she saw Bill, all the life left her body. This was where he worked, where he often slept. This is where she had called him to ask for his help.

At first, she thought the man with the jacket must have lied to her. He had just told her the name of the first place that came into his head. But the coincidence was overwhelming. Bill would have known that Mike was with Ana the night of the robbery. Bill would have known about the money. But Bill was supposed to be Ana's lover or at least her friend. Mike wrestled with thoughts of confronting him, of calling the cops and turning him in. But Ana cared about him. Ana would never forgive her, especially if Bill was innocent.

For the first time in more than a year, Mike went to a gay bar. She rarely drank, but she wanted to tonight. She needed to be with women, gay women, and she needed to be drunk.

The music was fast and too loud, the bar was smoky and too crowded, but Mike felt at home. She could walk her walk and feel her pride.

She wasn't used to sitting at the bar. In the past, she had always sat at a table with a lover or a crowd of friends. The

65

bar was the place for singles, loners, cruisers, and drinkers. She sat with her back to the eyes of a community that no longer recognized her. She listened to roles being played out around her: butches trying to be too cool, too tough; femmes hanging out in crowds to help them feel more secure.

She ordered wine. Though she preferred Lambrusco, anything red would do. The bartender was a tough old butch who kept feminine barmaids at her side and always knew when a customer needed someone to talk to.

"Hey, friend," the bartender said. "You all right? Looks like your arm is bleeding."

"Got into a fight on the East Side." Mike stuffed a napkin up her sleeve. "It'll stop soon."

A short blonde woman stepped up to the bar and ordered three beers. Mike gave her a half smile and turned back to her wine.

"What was someone like you doing on the East Side?" the blonde asked.

"Beats me," Mike answered.

The blonde took her beers to a table of friends and Mike gave the bartender a look that meant she thought the woman was cute.

"Not bad," the bartender said. "She's single, far as I know. My name's Cookie, if you need anything."

"I'll take another wine," Mike said. "And send three more beers over to that table."

The barmaid delivered the beers and pointed to the giver. Mike turned only slightly and toasted them with her wine. She laughed to herself as she remembered the old bars in California. The best way to find a single woman was to buy her a drink and toast her from afar. If she toasted back, she was single. If she ignored you, her lover was pretty close by and you might as well forget it.

The blonde only smiled and resumed talking to her friends. Mike went back to her wine and got lost in the music.

"Hello." The earth-mother voice brought Mike back to reality.

"Mag!" She gave Maggie a quick kiss. "What are you doing here? Where's Sheila?"

"Got a kiss for me, too?"

66

Jerking her head to her other side, Mike practically touched Sheila's nose with hers. "Not in here, I don't."

"What happened to you?" Maggie said. "I mean ... your arm is ... bleeding."

"I haven't heard that pause in your voice for weeks." Mike smiled. "This is nothin'. A little black dude was feeling a little cold today."

"Excuse me." A large black woman with glasses stepped between Mike and Maggie. "That's the second time tonight I've heard your racist remarks. First, the East Side. Now, some black dude. You got somethin' to say about black people, you say it to me."

"I don't talk about black people," Mike answered coolly. "Just assholes. Doesn't matter what color they are. If they're assholes, they're assholes."

"You sayin' I'm an asshole? 'Cause I'm black?"

"I ain't sayin' it. But if you start acting like one, I'll be sure to count you in."

They stared at each other for a full minute before Cookie tried to intercede. Mike waved her away and picked up her glass of wine.

"It's all right, Cookie. Me and my friend are just discussing the problems with the world. Black assholes, and white assholes. The world is full of 'em. Color's no excuse." She slowly sipped her wine while looking the other woman straight in the eye. "Wanna drink?"

The woman looked Mike over from head to toe and back again and raised her hand to put it on Mike's shoulder. Mike didn't flinch or bat an eye.

"You're all right," the woman said. A wide grin crossed her face as she warmly squeezed Mike's shoulder. "You're all right. You're a sister through and through. No doubt about it. Cookie, you give her another drink, on me."

She gave Mike's shoulder a final pat and sauntered off through the crowd. Mike felt all eyes on her. The whispering began instantly. Maggie resumed her position and Sheila took a seat on Mike's other side.

"That's the telephone game we're hearing now," Mike said. "By tomorrow, half the people here will swear there was a fight and they witnessed it all. The other half will swear they didn't hear a thing. By the time they're done, the story will be that some racist Italian butch tried to pick a fight with a black woman and it got all the nonracist white women very upset and the black woman was smaller and the white woman took advantage of that and the bartender had to throw them both out onto the street and isn't it terrible and no one they know would ever do anything like that."

"Would you like to dance off some of that wine, Mike?"

"Only if Sheila says so. I don't need any more fights today."

Sheila gestured her okay. Mike teetered a little when she stood up, but her manners were with her. Gracefully, she led Maggie through the crowd, past the eyes and the whispers, and onto the dance floor.

❑ ❑

"So, hoist up the John B sails. See how the main sails set. Call for the captain ashore, let me go home. I wanna go home. Please let me go home. I feel so broke up, I wanna go home."

Mike and Maggie sang together every time Mike could make it happen. They sang lesbian songs, favorites from the fifties and sixties, folk songs, and originals.

"Sharing music is kinda like making love." Mike felt almost childlike in her realization. Music had helped her become who she was and was both friend and foe. It was healing, it was hurtful.

"Yes," Maggie answered breathlessly. "It is. Especially when there's harmony."

"I guess that's why I always liked the Everly Brothers. The more they sang, the more I could make love to the women around me. Sometimes, I feel like I'm every song that was ever sung about a broken heart or a memory."

"Oh, Mike." Maggie put away her guitar and slid closer to hold Mike's hand. "I wish I ... could make it better."

Mike's hand almost fit inside of Maggie's, and it was warm, soothing, the kind of touch that makes broken hearts feel like melted wax. Mike looked at Maggie cautiously.

"It's okay," Maggie reassured. "Sheila and I have talked about it and it's okay."

The go-ahead given, Mike felt her history pull her up straighter and the strength she cherished slowly creep back into her being.

"You're sure?" Mike said as she carefully lowered Maggie to the floor beneath her.

"Yes. It's okay."

Mike lowered her gaze to Maggie's blouse and firmly unbuttoned the top two buttons. Maggie squirmed beneath her touch and began a gentle urging. Mike saw them as lovers on the silver screen, and Maggie's sense of drama played right into her fantasy. Maggie begged for Mike's touch, and then reassured her with her voice and the rhythmic sway of her body. She pulled Mike closer. As if trying to release all of Mike's butch parts that were still hidden inside, she begged for her hand, her mouth, her inner organ that would pound her and satisfy her.

"Do it to me, Mike. Make me come. I know you feel it inside of you. Do it harder. Harder!"

Mike moved her body as never before. She had to please. She felt as if her very soul was pushing her forward, making her become who she was supposed to be. She was a man, a woman, a father, a lover, a child, lost in the sudden eruption of fully grown sexuality.

I'm a butch. And I'm proud. And I love ... loving women. I'm a butch. I love it. And I love ... loving women. Over and over she repeated her inner chant. Again and again. Back and forth. Back and forth. Over and over. Maggie's body rocked beneath her as Mike moved above, arms straightened, pushing up, pushing in.

"Now, Mike! I'm going to ... I'm ... Yes! Oh, yes!"

"C'mon, baby," Mike cooed. "C'mon. Let it happen."

"Oh, God! Mike! I've never ... it's so ... ahh. So good. So good."

They collapsed against each other and Mike buried her face in the sweat between Maggie's breasts. They panted and touched and slept a little.

Mike's exhaustion caused her to dream and she envisioned herself in a small fishing boat rocking and crashing against angry waves. Ana was drowning and crying for help, but the waves hurled themselves against the boat, knocking Mike down, choking her, sucking the life from her body. She heard Amalia's cries and pulled herself to the edge of the boat to reach for her, but she was gone. The waves threw bits of paper into the boat and Mike struggled to read the words written on them. "Your song was the sweetest" was all she could see. With a silent scream, she reached frantically into the water again. Hands reached for hers from everywhere; hands with no faces, no bodies. They reached and begged and slid from her grasp. Sharon's voice called out to her. Leslie's hands dug into the side of the boat. The man with the knife slashed at the water. Ana's smile was in the mist and Sue looked down from somewhere above.

Mike jumped awake and held tightly to the woman beneath her. She opened her eyes and two very green eyes looked at her, whiskers tickled her nose. She lifted her head and looked toward the purring at her feet, then laid her head back on Maggie's breasts and listened to the sounds of hearts and breathing.

"Mag? Do your cats watch *everything* you do?"

"Only when Sheila's not around."

"Where is Sheila, anyway?"

"At work. She'll be home at nine-thirty."

Mike quickly checked her watch. "Mag, that's five minutes from now."

"Oh, no. We can't let her see us like this."

"I'm gone, Maggie. Gone! I'll talk to you tomorrow." She kissed Maggie quickly but passionately and raced outside to her car. She was sure she saw Sheila's headlights turn into her driveway. Mike pulled to the curb to pull herself together.

❏ ❏

My woman in America,

I feel something is happening with you and you don't want to tell me. Is it your health because you worry so? Something is keeping you from writing, and it makes me crazy not to know. Try to share it with me, baby. I need to know. I got a note from Bill and he says he misses me! What do you think about that? Amalia is waiting for your letters. My times are heavy.

I think I will always be with someone who is safe. I love you and can't wait to hear of my return.

❏ ❏

As summer turned to fall, Mike's job at the university grew increasingly more difficult. There were more computers to install, more communication lines to run, and more tense words with her boss than ever before. Women students and faculty dropped by her office constantly, and seven women on the staff complained to her about a man sexually harassing them.

She called Maggie a dozen times a day to laugh, to dream, to feel sane. They made love when Sheila was out, and sometimes, all three spent the night together in the same bed. It was friendly and nurturing and, at times, the perfect kind of peaceful.

Mike's passion for Maggie was constant and she always enjoyed her, but she felt no future, no commitment, no degree of power or territory that comes with knowing someone is only yours. Her allegiance lay with Ana and Amalia. She was their provider, the lover, the parent. She would give all she had for them, even her life if necessary.

Mike retreated even more from the community. In some ways, the women around her had been family, sisters and mothers and even some brothers. They were there when she began growing, and they helped to wean her from childish pleasures. They were constant and she knew them, but her secrecy with Ana, her relationship with Maggie, and the past that no one knew made her a runaway, a child who couldn't bear the judgment, the ridicule, the false assumptions, or the games.

Dear Ana,
I feel myself getting lost in the whirlwind of change. I try to hold on, to try to believe you love me, but I ache. I need you, now. I want you beside me and I need you. There was a time I thought I'd never say that, but it's lonely here. I cry out in the night because the memory of us tears at me, because my mind and my body need to wrap themselves around you and feel

your love. You know me. And sometimes I think you are the only one who truly understands me. But are you real? Will you be there when I come home? When I awake? Please tell me again because the distance is too great, the time too long. I need to believe in you and in us.

Dear woman,

I love you, love you, love you. There's no more for me to say. When I get there and am beside you, you'll know I'm real. For now, you have to trust me. I know you're lonely and I know the way your community destroys each other. They have forgotten that each of us has a history, a time before them, a time they know nothing about. They judge you for only the short time they've seen. It makes them important, or so they think. They are feminists and lesbians, women who love other women, but they hurt people like you and those they disagree with. They hurt you more than any man could. You must be strong and see where they're coming from. They're weak and scared, and like cats they scratch when they are cornered by someone whose life is deeper than theirs. I am always with you. I talk to you and hold you and feel the heat from you. If you need others to help you through, go to them. I'm not like other women you've known. Go to them and be with them. I will still be here.

❏ ❏

Renewed by Ana's commitment, Mike made a final attempt at securing her return. Because she traveled throughout the campuses repairing and installing computers, she knew many of the administrators. She'd often gone an extra step to make sure they were happier at work. Though she didn't like asking for favors, the time had come.

She went first to the Office of International Students.

"I have a friend who's trying to get into the Ph.D. program in Women's Studies," she said. "But she needs a special visa and some kind of statement from here."

Trusting Mike, the assistant answered, "I just need an acceptance from the department and the date she'll be starting."

"January," Mike answered. "I'll have her back, I mean, she should be back in time to start in January."

"Okay, Mike. If you can get me the acceptance letter ... or should I just call over for it?"

"No, no. I'll get it for you. They're always a little confused over there. You know, Women's Studies."

The assistant laughed. Mike was relieved that Women's Studies had a reputation for being slightly disorganized. She was also glad that she had department letterhead and could write the acceptance herself.

Mike went to the Graduate Students Office and crossed her fingers for luck. There wasn't a Ph.D. program, but Mike figured she could wing an acceptance as a student at the Office of International Students.

"It only says graduate student here, Mike. Does she have her master's?"

"Damn! They never get anything right. I'll take it back."

She looked at the assistant with pleading eyes.

"If she has her master's, then they must mean Ph.D.," the assistant said. "You're busy enough already. I'll just write it in and okay it."

Mike tried to hide her elation, but the tingling in her stomach seemed to reach up and make her smile wider than ever.

"When will I know?"

"Oh, this should go through in fourteen days. Then she takes it to her embassy. If they okay it, she's on her way."

"You're great!" Mike started to lean over to kiss the woman, but stopped herself in time. "Thanks! Thanks a lot. I'll tell your boss you deserve a promotion. Call me anytime you need something. I'll never forget."

She practically danced down the hall. Ana and Amalia would be back in no time. She called in sick for the rest of the day and sped home to call Chile. It would cost eight dollars a minute, but she had to tell Ana the news.

"*Ola!* I have news!"

"Be careful," Ana answered. "The phones. Remember the phones."

"I know, I know. Don't worry. The program at the university has accepted your application and issued you your papers. I'll be sending them to you in two weeks."

She waited for Ana's reaction.

"I don't believe it," Ana finally answered.

"You'll be home by Christmas, baby."

"I never thought it would happen. I should have known. I left it to you and I should have known you'd get it done. Oh, God! I don't know if I'll be ready!"

"You'll be ready. And so will I."

"Yes, yes. I know you will. By Christmas! Okay! I'll do it!"

Mike hung up and then immediately called Maggie at work.

"I just heard from Ana, Mag. They're coming home! Probably around Christmas!"

"Oh, Mike, that's ... great."

"It's been a year. Almost a whole year. Anyway, I have to cancel our date at the spa and also dinner this weekend. I want to make sure their apartment is clean and painted and stuff like that."

"Mike, they're not coming for two months."

Mike refused to let the slight resentment in Maggie's voice ruin the moment. "Doesn't matter, Mag. I have to do it."

"Why don't you wait until the weekend? Sheila might want to help you and—"

"I have to do this myself," Mike interrupted. "I've waited and waited, Mag. You have to understand how important this is to me."

"But I thought you told me you weren't sure if you trusted Ana. You told me you thought she was really straight. And what about her friend? Bill, is it?"

"She can't possibly go back to him, Mag. She knows he wouldn't help get her back here. She has to know what kind of asshole he is. And as far as her being straight goes, maybe she is, but most women I've been with were straight first. Her letters don't say she's straight."

"Well, I guess we'll talk when we can," Mag said sadly. "Bye, honey."

Mike knew Maggie was hurt. She had sensed a deepening need from her, a need for something more than a musical affair. She felt a little trapped again, but she couldn't back down now. Her family was coming home and she was more than ready to give them all the love they could handle.

She settled into the wavy black chair and hugged Amalia's favorite pillow. Looking around the room, she realized how empty it was. A cobweb clung to a far corner. Her green plants had turned brown. Through her window, above the building next door, she could just see the gray-blue sky and some clouds beginning to fill themselves with water. She hugged the pillow harder to stop the shaking that was overcoming her, but when the October rain began tapping on her windowsill, her tears pounded on her heart.

She scrubbed and painted, repotted and replenished both her home and Ana's. She called Maggie whenever she could. Their easy talk helped to mend any cracks in their friendship. She also called Ana's friends, instilling excitement in each as she told them of Ana's return. She wanted things perfect. Amalia would go back to a school where she would enjoy learning without the pressure or propaganda of military rule. Ana would also return to school, and Mike listed places she might find work. Things would be just as they had been.

Dear woman,

I spent the night shaking and worrying about my return to the U.S., my return to you. It scares me because I don't want people to know about us. It scares me because you have done so much and will expect so much. It's good that our houses are separate, but in the same building. It's good that we have kept up communication. But I feel guilty for all that I've asked, and it makes me tense. I'm writing to other friends to get travel money and I don't want you to say no. Others need the chance to do for me, not just you. I'm afraid of how we'll be when I finally get there, and if it doesn't work, I'll accept that. For now, take care.

Dear Ana,

Why are you doing this? After all we've been through, why do you choose now to reject me? I didn't mind doing all that I did. When you care for and love someone, you expect to do necessary things. Don't distance yourself. Not now when the time has finally come to erase the distance. I love you.

Dear Mike,

Please don't try to put a net around me. Always you build these webs and then it is you who are trapped. I need to have control of the one thing that is mine, my life. Friends have written and said they will send whatever I need. Friends have called and said they will be there to pick me up. When I come to you, we'll see what happens between us. Now I feel crazy, and I have much to do. Ana

❏ ❏

As October faded into the beginning of winter, Mike tried to maintain her faith in Ana. Things would work out. It was just the changes that were making Ana crazy. It was a process that they would work through together.

Dear Mike,

The embassy here has held up my papers. They give me no explanation. Is there something wrong with the things you sent? Did the university fill out the right forms? I can't believe I've readied myself to leave and now this is happening. Are you sure you did the right thing?

Mike's heart and mind filled with anxiety as she raced through all the steps she had taken for Ana's return. Letters took so long to arrive that she couldn't be sure if there was even more trouble by now. Everything seemed in order. She begged the Chilean embassy in New York for help. She haunted the American ambassador with desperate phone calls and letters.

76

Dear Ms. Landetti,

In response to your recent letters regarding case number 143526, we have been unable to find any discrepancy in channels. All paperwork seems to be in order and the required documents have been filed. We believe the delay is due to the upcoming Thanksgiving holiday. Once the regular staff returns to their posts it should take about two weeks for finalization. We hope this alleviates your concerns.

❏ ❏

Thanksgiving was one of the holidays Mike had promised to spend in Fredonia. Her father would make a turkey while her mother did crossword puzzles and then they'd vie for television time and fight about football. Al had grown mellower and seemed unwilling to participate in any quarrels, but Mike's mother, Fran, always maintained her position of authority. Mike played the role of dutiful daughter, but she refused to do dishes or act like a housewife. If her mother wanted her company, she intended to be just that: company.

A few aging uncles and one cousin showed up for dinner. No one talked about anything real, no one shared any real emotion. Mike always sat at the end of the table nearest her father and always dressed like a respectable butch. She knew she'd be the topic of conversation after she left, but she felt they had to deal with it. She didn't judge them or interfere with their lives. She expected the same in return.

When it was time to leave, Mike gave only passing kisses. It hurt. Maybe if they knew each other better, they could be more loving. But even love didn't seem to be the answer. It didn't always hold people together or make things easy or cause sunshine and rainbows. Most of the time, it didn't even feel good.

A snowstorm forced traffic to creep along the thruway. Mike blasted radio music to stay focused on her driving. Several times, she almost fell asleep and had to quickly roll down the window for a chilling burst of air. Her mind wandered to other winters. Only abrupt stops by cars ahead of her and flashing brake lights kept her from closing out the world.

If only her past had been different; if only she had made different choices. She wondered about the history people make for themselves and then realized that she really didn't know her parents' past. Children only know what they remember, and they seldom know anything about a mother's process or a father's pain.

Her father had made wrong choices. Instead of becoming a teacher, he had listened to his brothers and opened a restaurant. Instead of continuing to be a pilot after the war, he had washed dishes and tended bar. Then, he had fallen in love with an abused woman and dedicated his life to her.

Her mother came from a broken family on the other side of town. Alone and beaten, she had been forced to earn her way by waiting on tables at Al's restaurant. Eventually, Fran had divorced her husband and trusted the man who paid her. Al's compassion and love made him rebel against his Italian family. They had secretly married. Together they had made a child and named her after Al's buddy from the army.

"You were your father's queen," Mike's mother always said. "He didn't want kids until you were born, then you were all his, his pride and joy."

The restaurant had kept Fran and Al away more than twelve hours a day, so Mike had grown up with her god-mother, aunts, and baby-sitters. She'd only seen her parents when they were too tired to know her, too angry to understand her behavior.

Tears clouded Mike's eyes as she struggled to understand why things happened the way they did. Snow blew horizontally across her windshield, and ice on the wipers blocked her view. Mike remembered every beating from her father, every screaming match with her mother. She couldn't be their little queen; they couldn't resolve their anger at the choices they had made. Mike had grown up loving women, not because she chose to, not from some Freudian screw-up. It had come naturally, automatically, powerfully. Nature was her only guide and the one thing she most trusted.

As Mike matured, Fran had realized that her daughter's allegiance was to friends, not to family. The girls in Mike's life were important, and they were always there. When Mike had lost Sharon and hidden in the Fredonia cemetery to mourn, Fran had made a terrible decision, a choice. She had chosen survival. Fran had kicked Mike out of the house at the age of thirteen. She knew Mike would survive. She knew Mike's absence would give the rest of the family a better chance. She locked the door on Mike, and Al agreed.

It suddenly made some kind of sense to Mike. "Of course," she said to herself as she sat up alertly in the car, "that's why they did it!"

While she squinted for the exit sign that would take her safely off the thruway, she smiled a little at her new understanding. It didn't make it better, and it didn't make it go away, but she grew a little and healed a little. The tracks she made in the snow were just a little fresher.

❏ ❏

The following week, Mike bought the biggest Christmas tree ever. She purchased more lights and tinsel and spent hours making sure the decorations were perfect. She named the tree Amalia.

Dear Mike,

They say I should have my papers in two or three weeks. We should be flying into New York on January 3rd. Chilean friends will be meeting me there, so don't come. I'm not ready for any of them to know about us. We'll come to you in Buffalo, to your always warm house. Amalia is so excited! At last the problems are over.

Mike watered the tree every day and searched for remedies to keep it alive. Carefully she collected needles that were still green but unable to hold on. She arranged them in the shape of a Christmas tree on a special card and glued them into place.

Dear Amalia,

This tree is for you. It's waiting for you in my living room and it smiles every night when it thinks of you looking at it. I named it after you, squirt. See you soon.

On Christmas Eve, Mike went to church. It wasn't a ritual she thought necessary, and it didn't make her feel any closer to whatever God there was. But just in case, she went and prayed. She enjoyed the carols, the warmth, and even the make-believe friendship that people gave so freely. She knew going to church didn't really make anyone a better person. In fact, she believed that those who went regularly were the worst hypocrites, the real devils. But Christmas made all things, church included, seem better.

After the service, she walked the snowy streets buying coffee for everyone waiting at bus stops. She had placed a sign in the hallway of her building announcing an open house at her apartment. "For everyone with nowhere to go or no way to get there: food, drink, and a Christmas tree." When she arrived at her door, she was surprised to find a whole crowd of smiling strangers.

"I'm Jim from down the hall," one man said.

"And I'm Lucille from 2B."

An old woman with a cane waited with a package of cookies. "I'm Mrs. Tuttle from across the courtyard. My family is all gone. I always used to bake for them."

Mike opened her door as more people came down the hall.

"Don Lacy. From the other building."

"Beth and Tom. We live on the third floor."

And so it continued. Black and white, young and old, in pairs or alone. They mingled and ate and listened to carols. Some sat quietly, reflectively; others needed to let go with shouting and laughter. Mike played host until all were comfortable and then sat back on the wavy black chair and watched. She loved the way everyone admired the tree. They stayed through the night. Some dozed awhile, but most stayed wide-eyed, as if they thought they'd never see another Christmas and so wanted this one to last forever. Even old Mrs. Tuttle stayed until morning.

Mike made eggs, bacon, bagels, and fruit salad and told them all the house was theirs. A few left after promising to come back. Others stayed to help Mike make stuffing. By that afternoon, the turkey had been shared and the holiday survived by all. One by one, they left to get on with all the days that weren't Christmas.

❏ ❏

"We're having a New Year's Eve party and you're coming. No excuses, no sighs. Sheila and I expect you to help, so be there!"

When Maggie didn't wait for a reply, Mike knew it was something she had to do. Sheila and Maggie were just about her only friends. She owed them her attention.

Dressed in a black, tuxedolike outfit, Mike mustered all her butch pride before entering the party. It wasn't what she had expected. Maggie's house was full of couples: men and women from the library and neighbors from their street. Maggie wore a long, flowing dress and Sheila wore a frilly blouse. Mike felt completely out of place. She tried to get Maggie's attention to tell her she had to go home and change, but Maggie, busy with her audience, as usual, virtually ignored Mike's presence. Understanding Maggie's need for that kind of acceptance, her inattention didn't really bother Mike until almost midnight. As everyone started the countdown, Maggie readied a tape of "Auld Lang Syne." Mike's romantic heart flew to Chile at the first stroke of twelve, then flew back again to be hurt by the deep kiss Maggie gave Sheila. The guests, who all knew Maggie and Sheila were lovers, didn't bat an eye as the couple kissed. Mike was sad that those same partygoers couldn't also know that she and Maggie shared a special kind of loving.

A friendly man kissed Mike on the cheek. "Happy New Year," he said. Men seemed to gravitate toward her in emotional times. They sensed a camaraderie; there were no sexual undertones. If butches could fall in love with men, they'd probably make the best wives. Some men seemed to know that.

When the party was over, Mike returned home. Tonight was not to be shared. With only two days left before Ana and Amalia were to arrive in New York, she needed solitude and time to reflect.

Mike waited by the phone all day January 3rd. She wanted to be there in case there was a problem, in case the plane didn't leave Chile, in case it crashed. At 5 p.m., she called LAN Chile Airlines to make sure the plane had taken off on time.

"The plane took off right on schedule, sir."

"I'm not a sir," Mike said. "Can you check the manifest for the names, to be sure they got on the plane?"

"Yes, sir. We have both names on the manifest."

Ana and Amalia were due in at 9 p.m. At 10 p.m., Mike called New York to see if the plane had landed. Ana was supposed to call once she had cleared customs to let Mike know all was well.

"The plane landed five minutes late, but there were no problems."

She stayed off the phone to keep the line clear and turned on the television for a distraction. Something had to be wrong. She wished she hadn't listened to Ana. She wished she was in New York City greeting and hugging the people she loved.

By midnight, she began to panic. She had the airport page Ana, but no one answered the call. She called Ana's friends to see if they had heard from her, but no one answered the phone. She called Ana's parents in Chile to see what they had heard, but no one answered there, either. She paced. She smoked cigarettes, a habit she had given up. She drank coffee to stay awake and splashed her face with cold water to ease her dizziness.

When the sun rose, she called the airport to see if Ana had boarded a plane to Buffalo. Her name didn't appear on any manifest. Throughout the day, Mike made herself sick drinking coffee, smoking cigarettes, pacing, and shaking. When the phone rang at 5 p.m., she grabbed at it so quickly that the receiver flew through the air. She retrieved it and waited breathlessly for a voice.

"Hello? Hello?"

"*Ola.*"

"Oh, thank God! Where are you? Are you here? Jesus Christ, where have you been?"

"I'm here. Upstairs at my beautiful house."

"Here? Why didn't you come to my apartment first? Why didn't you tell me? I'll be right up!"

"Wait. We're very tired and people are here. Amalia almost didn't make it. Because she was born here she needed a special visa that you didn't think of. We'll come to breakfast tomorrow and talk then."

"Can't I just come up to say hello?" Mike pleaded.

"It'll be better tomorrow."

Mike hung up and then mechanically went to the kitchen to get water for the Christmas tree. It was slowly dying and some of its branches were so dry that the slightest touch made them snap and crumble. Still, it was Amalia's tree, and she had promised to keep it until she arrived.

Her arms felt numb and the heaviness on her shoulders made her walk with unsure steps. Without thinking, she went to her bedroom, grabbed a pillow and a blanket, and shuffled to the couch. The back of the couch felt good against her body. She curled into it like a cat, warm, hugged, and safe.

Mike opened her eyes to a foggy morning. The light tapping at her door felt like hammering inside her head. Still dressed from the night before, she ran a finger across her teeth and pushed back her hair.

"*Ola,* Mike!" Amalia stood in front of Ana holding up a handmade card. "We're back!"

"Hi, squirt." Mike's voice was barely audible. She forced a smile as she glanced at a silent Ana. Amalia tugged at her shirt to get her attention and then pointed to the floor.

"Oh, yeah," Mike said. "I almost forgot."

When Mike got down on one knee, Amalia jumped into her arms. It took Mike a moment to return the hug. She surprised herself with her caution.

"See what's in the corner?"

"The tree! Mama, *mida,* look! I told you it would be here! My mom didn't believe me. She thought the tree would be gone by now, but I told her you promised."

"There's stuff under it too." Mike warmed to Amalia's elation. "Santa told me to hold onto them for you."

Amalia ran to the presents as Ana inched her way through the door.

"*Ola,*" Ana said with only half her mouth.

Mike opened the door wider and Ana moved closer for a cheek kiss.

"Mama! Look at all the stuff Santa Mike bought!"

"Amalia, let Mike show you what is yours. Don't be greedy."

"It's all hers," Mike said. "Let her have fun. It's Christmas Day for her."

"She's learned to live without all this stuff," Ana answered. "I don't want her to get greedy."

Mike headed for the kitchen. She didn't want their first minutes together to be filled with quarrels.

"How about potato pancakes for breakfast? And fruit?"

Ana sat sideways on the black chair watching Amalia tear at wrapping paper. "Do you have kiwi?" she asked.

"Uh, no. It's not in season. I have just about everything else."

"Whatever. We're not so hungry early in the morning."

"Oh, yeah. I forgot. Lunch is the big meal. *Quiere, cafe?*"

Mike smiled and winked at Ana. It had been one of the first questions Ana had asked Mike when they had begun their friendship.

"Si." Realizing Mike's joke, Ana finally looked at her with a softer face. "Yes, I'll have coffee."

They ate, made small talk, and avoided each other's eyes. Mike didn't know what to think of Ana's behavior. She tried to make her smile, tried to make her angry, tried to ignore her. But Ana's response was constant silence. After an hour and a lot of unfinished breakfast, Ana took Amalia's hand and told her it was time to go.

"But I wanna stay and see Mike. And my presents. I wanna play, by the tree!"

"You'll have plenty of time to see Mike. We have to unpack and get settled."

Mike watched them walk hurriedly down the hall and disappear up the stairwell. Every bit of her wanted to race after them and smother them with all her pent-up love, but she didn't. Instead, she waited a reasonable length of time before calling Ana on the phone.

"I thought maybe we could talk now that Amalia can't hear."

"Not now. I'm tired and—"

"Too tired to say something nice? Or friendly?"

"I am friendly to you, but I'm tired."

"Why don't I come up and help you unpack?"

"You can't right now, I have company."

"Oh." At first, Mike thought Ana just needed some space while she visited with all her Chilean friends. She was probably exhausted and overwhelmed after her long trip. Then, she realized what was going on. "It's Bill, isn't it?"

"Yes."

"How long has he been there? Since last night? Did he meet your plane too?"

"No, he didn't meet me. He came over after I got home."

"Did you call him?"

"Yes."

Mike felt her hand crushing the receiver. She wanted to rush upstairs, throw Ana on her bed, and love her as only a butch could. She wanted to make her see what she was about to lose. Instead, she simply hung up.

It was three days before Ana showed up at her door. She walked in with hardly a knock, smiling, joyful, full of energy. Mike didn't know how to react. All she knew was that if Ana wanted any part of her now, she would have to offer a damn good explanation and do a lot of apologizing. But Ana did neither. She had nothing to give but meaningless talk. Finally, Mike had enough. She grabbed Ana's wrist tightly, enough to know it hurt her.

"Why are you doing this to me? What the hell did I do to you to make you do this?"

"I am doing nothing." Ana didn't pull away or resist.

"That's just it. I thought we were ... I thought we had something together. All those words. All those feelings."

"You still have it. You just don't know that you do."

"What the hell does that mean? Why do you always have to talk to me in some kind of code?"

Satisfied that they could were going to talk things out, Mike let go of Ana's arm.

"You try to draw a net around me," Ana said. "You wrote only about the things you did for me and it made me feel no one else here cared."

"Not no one. Just assholes like Bill."

"I felt like it was no one. And you try to trap me, pull me into your net. I can't be like that."

Ana opened the door to leave but turned when Mike spoke.

"It wasn't a net, it was love. I asked you to tell me the truth about us. I trusted you. Bill didn't want anything to do with getting you back. Only the people who truly love you did anything to help. I trusted you." Mike couldn't hold back her tears. Her lower lip quivered like a child's, and an awful sob contorted her face.

"I trusted you," she continued. "You made me believe you loved me and we would be together."

"I didn't lie. I just can't have it the way you think it should be."

With that, Ana closed the door and was gone.

Mike broke each branch off the Christmas tree and stuffed the limbs into garbage bags. The tree was so dry that it took two hours to sweep and vacuum up the needles. Each branch was like a day. Each needle, a tear.

Ana called regularly, but their conversations were tense and shallow. One morning, Mike decided to give it a last try. She knew if she could just hold Ana for a minute and show her the love that awaited her, everything would be okay. Still in her robe, Mike climbed the stairs and gently knocked on Ana's door. When Ana answered, she was fully dressed and ready to go out. She hardly looked at Mike as she finished fixing her hair and preening in the mirror.

"Good morning. You look like you just got up."

"You look like you've been up for hours. It's only six-thirty!"

"Bill is coming to take me to breakfast and Amalia's gone to school already!"

"Just thought I'd come up to say hi," Mike said. "I guess I'll leave you alone."

"See you!"

Ana went back to her preening. Mike went back to her couch.

❏ ❏

With the cold days of winter slowly ending, Mike decided to get back into the community. She chose the Women's Studies department as a starting point. She was familiar with the program, she already knew many of the women in the department, and she could teach there again on a part-time basis. She tried her best to be outgoing, but every woman she befriended either thought Mike was courting her or wanted more from Mike than she was able to give.

"It's not fair, Mag. Butches aren't allowed to just be friends with anyone, you know? Femmes think they're flirting, other butches worry about competition, and the ones who don't think they're into role-playing try to turn butches into men."

Maggie finished setting up her tape recorder and then positioned herself on the couch with her guitar. "I think butches are wonderful," she said, almost too sweetly. "They've fought and paved the way so women can love each other. We couldn't live without them."

"Besides," Mike teased, "they make better lovers." She played with a tambourine and some drumsticks, and together they reshaped their music.

Tryin' to love two women, is like a ball and chain.
Tryin' to love two women, is like a ball and chain.
Sometimes the pleasure ain't worth the strain.
It's a grand old drag, and it tires my mind.

Sheila surprised them both by joining them in the living room with a bass guitar.

"Self-taught," she said. "I wanna play too."

"Sheila! This is great. Okay, let's try this. You and Mike know 'Sister, Sister,' right?"

The duo became a trio, and through the music, they learned each other's fears and dreams and hidden places. Maggie's music was almost an obsession for Mike. She wanted Maggie onstage, sharing her words and her voice, healing and teaching the women who would love her. They weren't yet good enough to play in public together, but Maggie had always been good enough, and Mike wouldn't let her waste her time.

"They want you at Greenfield Street Restaurant and you're going." Mike wouldn't take no for an answer. She lugged speakers, guitars, and tape recorders to every concert, and she sat in front so Maggie could see her and so she could protect Maggie from any rejection from the crowd.

Slowly, she became a manager and a "straight man," the loudest laugh and the longest applause. The banter between them warmed the audience and made each concert seem more personal. The more they shared, the more they made love. And the more they made love, the more Mike worried that their relationship was not okay with Sheila.

"Dina's coming to rehearsal today," Maggie announced as she met Mike and Sheila for a practice session. "She plays guitar and has a pretty good voice, so we thought we'd see how it worked."

"She's going to sing?" Mike asked.

"Sometimes." Maggie casually tuned her guitar. "Don't worry. You'll still have your parts."

Mike toughened up her stance as soon as Dina entered the room. She wanted to make sure Dina knew whose turf she was on, but she also had to be careful about Sheila's territory. Whenever Sheila glanced Mike's way, Mike lowered her shoulders and softened her glare. But, as soon as Sheila looked away, she flexed her arms and fixed her eyes on Dina. In some ways, she was trying to protect Sheila, too. Somehow she felt it was okay that she and Maggie were having an affair, but she knew it was wrong for Dina to step in. Sheila wasn't the kind of butch Mike was. She was more laid back, more middle class. Mike wasn't sure Sheila could fight if she had to, so Mike decided to fight for her.

Their first concert together as "Maggie Romano and Friends" was a casual affair, but Mike was so nervous she couldn't breathe. Her job was percussion and vocals. It took the ending of the first number and feeling the applause to realize she had actually done it. Her eyes scanned the crowd. Leslie sat in the audience with friends they had shared. Women from the college waved at each other. Women who wanted Mike as a lover looked up at her with adoring smiles. The enemies who always caused division in the community whispered and snickered in the front-row seats. They were all there: the people who always judged, those who listened to the judges, and the few still innocent.

It was time for Maggie's debut song, a song she had written for Mike after one of their long talks about Chile and lovers and being a butch.

Down the road she traveled on a dark and dusty
*   evening*
While her shadow followed purple
through the narrow winding vale.
She was dressed in leather breeches,
and her hair was short and slickered.
And she looked like any outlaw on the trail.

I had heard of her in stories,
and in songs the men were singin'
when the women weren't allowed to listen in.
Oh, they said she was a bandit,
and she lived by robbin' bankers.
But most of all they said
that her existence was a sin.

But I dreamed, of the gentlin' of her hands
And I dreamed, of the firelight in her eyes
That I'd ride along beside her and go anywhere
*   she'd take me.*
And I'd live the life she loved until I die.

I was walkin' by the stream that runs through my
*   daddy's homestead.*
When I saw a dark and lonely figure ridin' through the
*   trees*
She said, "Lady, don't be frightened, for I have not
*   cóme to harm you.*
But my horse and I are thirsty. May we share your
*   water, please?"*

Oh, her voice was low and calming, and we smiled as
*   she dismounted*
And she quenched their thirst with water, as she told
*   me where she'd been.*
In my life I knew I'd never had this feelin' that was
*   stirrin'*
And the sweet touch of her fingers told my heart this
*   was no sin.*

And I knew, by the gentlin' of her hands
And I knew, by the firelight in her eyes

That I'd ride along beside her and go anywhere
she'd take me
And I'd live the life she loved until I died.

I cried, "Please to take me with you, for I know now
that I love you."
She said, "Darlin' there's a danger if you leave with me
tonight.
I'm an insult to the rich folk, takin' money, lovin'
women."
But I paid no heed to warnin' and we rode in the dusky
light.

And the town called out a posse, sayin' that I had been
kidnapped
And before the morning sun they found us sleepin'
'neath the sky.
Well, they shot her without warning, in my arms she
lay there bleeding
Whisperin', "Lady, know I love you," in the breath
before she died.

And I swear, by the gentlin' of her hands
And I swear, by the firelight in her eyes,
That I'll ride along without her, and go where her spirit
leads me.
And I'll live the life she loved until I die.

The discriminating crowd burst into thunderous applause. Mike felt proud. She knew most of the audience didn't know the origin of the song, and it really didn't matter. As long as it stirred something in their souls, gave them a vision of the women who had come before them, she was satisfied.

❏ ❏

Maggie and Mike continued to see each other as often as time allowed, but Maggie was also having private rehearsals with Dina and Mike couldn't show her jealousy. Besides, she never believed Maggie would leave Sheila for her, though Maggie tried to indicate that at times. Maggie told her she wanted a relationship, but she didn't say it would be monogamous and Mike thought she needed that commitment.

"Cassie's going to join the band," Maggie said. "She's a marvelous fiddler! I think she'll add a lot. And besides, she's very cute."

Cassie was a short Irish girl with long, flowing hair. Mike had seen her a few times, maybe even spoken to her, but she was straight and no threat to anyone in the group.

The five of them rehearsed and cried and laughed and screamed and played and sang, always doing justice to Maggie's music, always tying the songs to women's lives.

People in the Buffalo community also got together. They wondered who was sleeping with whom, if Sheila knew, if Dina's lover knew, if Cassie had come out. They couldn't wait to see a performance so that they could form their own conclusions.

Mike convinced Maggie that her music should be on a record, and a date was set for a fund-raising concert. Hundreds of tickets were immediately sold, and posters for "Maggie Romano and Friends" were distributed everywhere.

"Mag, I'm so nervous."

"Oh, honey. You'll be fine. We sound wonderful!"

"But all those people!"

"You can't see that far anyway. All you'll see is the lights. Besides, I'll be right there next to you. I'm the one with all the solos! If anyone should be nervous it's me!"

"You've done this for years."

Maggie rubbed Mike's naked back and tried to soothe her. "Look, it'll be just like rehearsal and we'll have a good time. You've got three weeks to get it out of your system."

The weeks went by too quickly for Mike. She rushed around trying to find the right clothes and cursed Buffalo for not having stores like New York or L.A. Pressure from outsiders mounted as they struggled to become important to anyone in the band. Rumors went with every new ticket, and Mike finally locked herself away for the final days. She didn't want to be in the community headlines. She hated the power wielded by those who called themselves leaders, and she scorned those who followed without question and were afraid to disagree. She was hated by some because they thought she had cheated on Leslie. She wasn't trusted because no one knew what her relationship to Ana meant. She never told her side of the story or defended herself. To her it was more important for Leslie to feel support and for Ana to maintain her secrecy. Even Maggie needed to feel accepted, and Mike was willing to let her say or do whatever she had to to survive.

The night of the concert, Mike took hot baths every two hours. She still couldn't keep herself from shaking.

"Thank God Maggie's going to be there," she said to a friend. "If we have our normal banter, I might live through this."

Ana and Amalia didn't say they were coming, but Mike knew they probably would. She had hoped they would come down and wish her good luck, but they didn't.

An hour before the concert, the phone rang. Mike smiled. "So they are calling me," she said to herself.

"Mike? Maggie. Don't come over here. We'll meet you at the church."

"Why? What's wrong?"

"It's Sheila. She just got all freaked out about you and me. She says she's going to kill you."

"She's just nervous about the concert, Mag."

"No, Mike. Believe me. She's so angry, she tore the banister off the wall and was on her way to your house to use it on you. Just meet us there."

Mike parked her car at the church and carried her drums, kazoos, and tambourine through the already crowded hall. Backstage, Maggie was sitting with Dina on one side and Sheila on the other. Mike tried to say "Hi," but they ignored her. When Cassie arrived, Mike finally got a nod and a welcome, but Cassie was visibly shaken by the tension and retreated to her own corner.

Mike was terrified and confused. She had arranged much of Maggie's music, and she and Dina would be sharing vocals. They were situated onstage so that Maggie separated her from Sheila and Dina, but they were a band. They had to look at each other, feel each other, join together to make it right.

When they were finally introduced and walked up on-stage, all Mike could feel was anger. She knew the show had to go on, but she couldn't smile, couldn't interact with the crowd, and couldn't get support from Maggie. Even when Maggie somehow forgot that she wasn't supposed to speak to Mike and they started to play a little between numbers, the glares from Sheila snapped them back to reality. Mike felt completely destroyed. She knew that Maggie's music could mean so much; it could heal and give pride and stop division. But there were those in the community, and there always seem to be, who felt unimportant and used the occasion to gain some significance. They had pressured Sheila, warned Maggie, spread rumors, and sat in judgment.

When the three hours was finally over, the band received a long standing ovation. They had been great in spite of everything. They had blended for Maggie's sake, for music's sake, and for the sake of the women who listened. They had all planned to go out to a bar and celebrate. Mike drove her own car and entered alone. Maggie's table was full of the rest of the band and a few assorted friends.

"I need to talk to you, Mag," Mike pleaded.

"Not now, Mike. Sheila will go crazy."

"Well, what about me? What about if I go crazy? What about me, damn it?"

"Maybe tomorrow," Maggie whispered. "I'll call you."

Mike almost crawled out of the bar. She drove herself home and went into her house to sit in the dark. She knew why Sheila felt the way she did. She wanted credit for being the lover of the star, and Mike wouldn't have minded that. She didn't need that kind of significance. But she did need people to know she was a person, with a history and feelings just like theirs.

"Fuck this," she said the next morning. She dressed in her tightest jeans and blackest shirt. There'd be no more relationships, no more broken homes. She'd date until she found the right person, just like straight people did, and then she'd settle down.

NON-MONOGAMY

At the end of the next week, Mike heard that the band was going out of town for a concert and she made sure she was in front of Maggie's house to send them off. She just wanted to see the look on their faces when she showed up. Everyone but Cassie ignored her.

"Sorry you're not coming," Cassie said shyly. "It'll be different without you there."

"I'm glad you realize that," Mike answered as she glared at the car.

"They realize it, too. They just won't admit it."

"Well, I don't really want you to flop, because it wouldn't be fair to the audience, but I can't say I hope you're great."

"I guess I understand." Cassie looked at her with soulful eyes as the group in the car beeped for her to hurry.

"Go on," Mike said. "You don't have to feel sorry for me. I wouldn't want to go now anyway. Go on. Break a leg."

"That's not what I'm feeling, but ... I guess I should go."

Mike wanted to shoot them her middle finger as they drove away, but she still loved Maggie and she wasn't mad at Cassie. She thought it strange that they were going off to sing songs about how wonderful it is to be gay, and sisterhood, and dykes having fun.

She roamed the streets in her car checking for reactions from people she knew and people who were at the concert. Most seemed like they didn't really care, and a few glared at her in silence. She decided Emma's bookstore was a good place to gauge reactions. Besides, she needed some new books on vitamins.

"I'm looking for something on B vitamins," she said to Jackie. "I don't know if it's stress or what, but I'm too young to be getting any gray hair and I've got a few."

"I don't really follow vitamins. Guess you can tell by my gray hair, right?"

As Jackie laughed at her own joke, Mike enjoyed her smile. It didn't seem like Jackie was involved with the gossips, or what Mike now called the "leaders of destruction." She was easygoing. Mike liked that. She seemed like the kind of woman Mike could fall in love with, but not now.

"This is what we've got," Jackie said. "You're welcome to look."

Mike scanned the few titles Emma's store carried and checked for other references. She ordered two books, paid up front, and made sure she smiled when she thanked Jackie.

When she got home she was surprised to find a once familiar face at her door.

"Hi, Mike. Still got your TV?"

She let Amalia in, marveling at her ease. Children were much better at living life the way it was meant to be. They got angry, but just for a moment. They told the truth, even if it hurt. And they always knew how to make up, even if they weren't the ones fighting.

"Wanna come up for dinner later? My mom said I could ask you."

"Maybe, squirt. I don't know if your mom and I can get along yet."

"Hmm. I've been asking her what's wrong, but she won't say. Then I ask her how come you've changed so much and she says to ask you. So?"

"So. So, I don't know. Sometimes people just can't talk to each other and it hurts them. Somewhere between Chile and Buffalo, your mom and I forgot how to talk."

Amalia yawned dramatically and rubbed her eyes.

"You tryin' to tell me something? Or are you just tired?"

"It's the tea," Amalia said. "You know, the tea bag thing."

"Keep goin', kid, I don't know what you're talkin' about."

"I had a cup of tea this morning and my mother wouldn't let me go to sleep. Got it?"

"Uh, no. What does tea have to do with sleeping?"

"C'mon, Mike. It says right on the tea bag. Add hot water and sleep for ten minutes."

Mike got a tea bag from her cupboard and read the directions.

"Was it this kind? It says add hot water and *steep* for ten minutes. Steep, squirt, not sleep."

"Ohhh. Well, then I guess I'm not tired. Except, what does *steep* mean?"

"To let it soak in hot water."

"Okay, I got it."

Mike suddenly realized that Amalia was playing a game with her, the kind of game Amalia and other kids were very good at. She was trying to tell Mike something without upsetting her and she had found the perfect example.

"Does your mom have trouble reading things the right way?"

"All the time."

"And have I steeped long enough?"

"Maybe a little too long." Amalia grinned from dimple to dimple and Mike felt a tingle in the middle of her chest.

"It still won't be easy, kid. We've said a lot of things, felt a lot of pain, done all the things grown-ups do to make them look like silly kids. It'll take a while before we can be friends again."

"I know. One time I had this really great friend at school, or at least I thought she was. Then one day, out of nowhere, she stopped talking to me. The more I tried, the worse it got. Finally I just gave up. As soon as I quit trying, she came up and started talking to me again. It seemed like it took forever.

I hope you still like rice and stuff, 'cause that's what Mom's makin'."

"I didn't say I'd go."

"Please? Pretty please?"

"How can I resist?"

Dinner was tense, but at least a beginning. Ana and Amalia were playful and Mike enjoyed their laughter, but she couldn't help pulling back whenever it seemed like things were getting like they used to be. She wanted to ask about Bill. She wanted to run away and take them with her. She wanted to feel some kind of calmness, some kind of peace.

"Why do you do this to yourself? Do you know what you do?"

Mike only shook her head. She wanted Ana to tell her, but she didn't want to hear it.

"You make people dependent on you, draw them in with your strength. Then they get stronger and leave you."

"That's bullshit," Mike replied quietly. "I don't make people do anything; they decide."

"Oh, Mike. Why can't you see it? You were with Leslie during her most crucial times. You gave her everything, including your strength. She was strong enough to make her own decisions and to leave you.

"You made Maggie stronger, so she felt more important, more special. You made her love you, and you made her afraid to love you. With me, it's the same thing. You tried to give me your life. You did everything for me. You gave so much there was nothing left. Then, when you're drained of all strength, all energy, you want that other person to love you more than ever. They can't. You have to live for you. Make your life everything it should be."

"I don't believe that, Ana. When you love someone, you should give them everything, every part of you. I think everyone holds back too much. We're afraid to tell someone we love them. No one tells their neighbor, no one tells their friends. It's like everyone's too afraid of the one emotion we should be happiest to show. No. You give me too much power. The women I've been with were strong already, just like you. All I did was love them enough so they could use that

97

strength, feel that power. If that's bad, then I want to stay bad."

"Then you will stay unhappy. That's all there is to it."

"Maybe so. But a lot of women will be happier."

"Read Shakespeare. You turn the knife slowly. People don't know that kind of love and it cuts them."

"Did it cut you? Didn't it get you back here where you wanted to be?"

"No! This you must understand! If I came back later, or never made it back, it would have been better than what happened. You made me love you so much I tortured myself until I had to make your memory go out of mind so I could survive. When I couldn't love you the same way you loved me, it hurt you. That tortured me even more."

Mike thought about Ana's statement and quickly flashed on all the people she had loved before. "So," she answered a little sadly, "you were really no different. You have to love safely, just like everyone else. Not too much commitment, not too much caring, not someone who will love you enough to make you do that."

Now it was Ana's turn to think, but Mike knew she was right. That's why Ana stayed with a jerk like Bill. He was married and a loser. It was safe to love him, because she would never have to love him very deeply. She wouldn't get hurt.

Mike got up to leave and gently kissed Ana on the cheek. "Look at your daughter. She loves without fear." She paused to make her image stay in Ana's eyes. "You don't know what you threw away."

"And you don't know that it will always be," Ana answered.

❏ ❏

The dating game began casually with a phone call to Dina's ex-lover. Shari and Dina had broken up when Dina started practicing with Maggie. Mike had always liked her, but she wasn't looking for anything more than a nice dinner and uncomplicated conversation.

Mike dressed a little softer than usual and took Shari to a cozy Italian restaurant she knew would cater to them. It wasn't an easy night. Shari immediately assumed that Mike was after something she didn't want to give and so she avoided talking about anything personal. When Mike dropped her off at home, she knew they would never go out again. Shari had heard too many rumors and made too many assumptions about Mike. It was sad. They could have stayed friends.

Mike joined the teaching collective at the college to at least keep her in touch with her politics. Most of the women were younger and not in touch with their sexuality, but some of the older women showed Mike respect. She needed that. She had been out for almost twenty years and appreciated the fact that some women were willing to learn from her.

The meetings were always long and hard. They discussed class differences, racism, sexuality, and women's history. The young disagreed with the old, whites patronized those of color, gay women had to teach straight women about their repressed sexuality, and the younger lesbian-feminists thought they knew everything there was to know about being gay.

"There's no such thing as roles," Myra said. She was eighteen and had just come out through the women's movement and the university. "If we follow roles we're copying men and women."

Sal, a twenty-year-old from New York, nodded. "I agree. To me, a butch is someone who's trying to be a man. And calling someone a femme is degrading."

Mike held her tongue. She knew understanding came slowly and only after a great deal of time, talking, and that special thing called process. She wished it was easier. She wished she didn't have to be the one to speak up or try to explain. It seemed like younger lesbians were always trying to negate history, to reinvent lesbianism. She respected their process, but she couldn't control her frustration over the differences between street dykes and movement lesbians.

"My lover and I are equals," said Myra. "We share each other's clothes and do the same work at home."

"But who starts when it's time to make love?" Mike interrupted.

"What? I don't know what you mean. We both start."

"Really? No one does the seducing? No one leads?"

"No. We switch. Sometimes I want her, and sometimes she wants me."

"And what about when you want each other at the same time?"

"I don't understand."

"Who's on top?" Mike said, slowly and softly. "Who makes sure the other is satisfied? Who drives? Who deals with men differently than straight women do? Who can't pass for straight? Who doesn't have a choice?"

"A choice?"

"To be gay?"

"I really don't appreciate this," said Sal. "My partner and I can both pass for straight if we want to and we both came out in the first women's studies class we ever took."

"I don't like it either," Myra added. "Just because *you* choose not to wear makeup or girl's clothes doesn't mean you're right. You choose to look like a boy and act like a man, and that's what's wrong with role-playing. Seems to me it's like playing house. One's a man and one's the little woman."

The room went silent. Mike thought about what Myra and Sal had said. She tried to find reasons for their feelings and she tried to control her anger.

When she was ready to speak, she stood up. "I feel sorry for you. I don't know what makes you so afraid. Afraid of that special part of a culture you have chosen to be a part of."

She looked directly at Myra. "Maybe the reason you and your lover share clothes and makeup and whatever is that you're both femmes. Maybe you just now, through the college, found out that it's okay to love another woman. That every woman isn't competition. Maybe you're really not gay at all. Maybe it felt so good to finally be allowed to care for other women that you decided you *must* be gay."

She let her words sink in before turning her gaze to Sal.

"And I especially feel sorry for you. You have such contempt for those who've come before you. If dykes hadn't worn jeans, you wouldn't have them on now. And as far as the playing-house thing goes, men and women are the ones who *play* house, not dykes. Men do a few dishes, mow the lawn while tanning their chests, get laid when they want to, and have all the power money can buy. Dykes, butches and femmes, can't do that. They don't have the same freedom or power. But you know what? That's okay, because we have something straight people will never understand. We know how to love each other with a passion no man can equal, with a power money can't buy. And when we play, we don't pretend to be grown-ups. We remember every special part of childhood that let us be free. We roll and romp and laugh and even cry with a freedom no straight man or woman will ever have."

She straightened her papers and tossed her jacket over her shoulders. "The sad part is that many of you are telling others that you're lesbians, women who love women, when you're really women who still hate every woman who's not like you, every woman who competes for attention. Experiment, if you have to. Learn, because you need to. But don't tell me and the butches and femmes who come after me that we don't exist or that we're wrong or that we don't know how to be lesbians. When you do that, you cut my soul. And I can't let you do that. Remember something," she said, pointing her finger at Myra and Sal, "I'm the fear that made your mother marry your father. Without me you wouldn't be here."

She added two fingers to the pointing one and tapped all three against her chest. "Maybe someday you'll know what this means."

❏ ❏

A collective member named Rachel shouted after Mike as she stormed out of the meeting. "Wait! I want to talk to you." Mike didn't stop. When her anger peaked, she knew it was best to be alone. Besides, Rachel probably just wanted to argue some more. Mike got into her car and sped past Rachel's wave. She started to head for the thruway to Fredonia, but made a U-turn and went home instead. Ana was waiting near her door when she got there.

"Oh, good. I need a ride."

"Well, let's go. I got nothing else to do."

Ana recognized Mike's need to be silent and so they drove in friendly quiet. When they got back home, Ana invited her up for tea.

"I don't think I'm very good company," Mike said. "Maybe another time."

"Be careful," Ana said as Mike walked away. "Protect yourself."

The phone was ringing when Mike opened her door, but she didn't want to answer it. When it continued long past twelve rings, she answered it with a very loud "What!"

"Is that any way to talk to an old friend?"

"Marge?"

"Right! I've been calling all day. Aren't you ever home?"

"I guess not. Where are you calling from?"

"Washington. I have to come to Buffalo this weekend and I wondered if I could stay with you."

Mike hesitated. Marge was an old friend from Women's Studies. She was middle class, a little flighty, and always seemed to be flirting. "I guess so. I only have one bedroom."

"That's okay. If it's okay with you, that is."

"Yeah, sure. How long are you going to be here?"

"Just a couple days. I've kinda had it with Washington and I wanna check out moving back to Buffalo."

"Suit yourself, my friend. If I didn't have to be here, I'd be long gone."

Mike agreed to pick up Marge at the airport and hung up just as someone knocked on her door. Cassie stood in the hallway looking puppy-eyed and sighing.

"What's wrong?" Mike asked.

Cassie only sighed again. Mike hated it when she asked a direct question and got sighs or silence in return.

"Well, the door's open. Come in if you want. Do what you have to do. I need coffee."

Cassie came in, leaving the door open behind her. She shuffled through the living room to the kitchen, stopped in the doorway, and sighed again. Mike didn't want to play the game.

"Either talk or sigh quieter," said Mike.

After another sigh, Cassie finally answered. "The band is breaking up."

Mike waited for more explanation, but Cassie wasn't about to give it without prodding. "That's it? That's what all this drama is about?"

Cassie nodded and slumped against the doorway.

"Do you want to tell me why?" Mike asked. "Or am I supposed to guess? Let me see, you went to Syracuse and the concert was pretty good, but Maggie was depressed about it, right?"

"Kinda. We really weren't very good and we really missed the percussion. I said something about the difference in the sound and Sheila got angry and Maggie cried and the whole thing was a mess."

Mike felt a little sorry for Cassie. She had been a musician all her life and playing good music was important to her. She didn't know what to do to make her feel better. They were friends because they shared a love for music. Cassie was questioning her sexuality, and she and Mike had fooled around a little, but they really didn't know each other very well.

"Wanna go for ice cream?" Mike asked. Cassie's face lit up like a child's. "Hold on while I see if the kid wants to go, too."

She called upstairs and Amalia met them at the outside door. Cassie looked a little disappointed that Amalia was joining them, but Mike always made the kid a priority. Cassie would have to accept that. When they got to the corner, Rachel was sitting at the bus stop. She gave a little wave, and Mike asked her to join them.

"No, thanks. I don't need any ice cream." She patted her stomach and puffed out her cheeks to make her point.

When the trio came back from the soda shop, Rachel was still on the bench.

"Didn't the bus come yet?" Mike asked.

"I wasn't waiting for the bus."

"Oh. Okay. None of my business."

Mike made sure she stopped at the outside door as a signal to Cassie that it was time for her to leave.

"Feel better?"

Cassie sighed again and Mike put a gentle arm around her shoulder. "There'll be other bands. Everything will be okay."

Mike left her outside and then sent Amalia upstairs. Again the phone rang as she opened her door. This time it was Maggie.

"Hello." Maggie's dramatic whisper caught Mike off guard. "I want to see you."

All the pain from the concert came back to fill Mike's body. "What about Sheila?"

"She works nights for the next two weeks. Do you think we could ... talk?"

"I don't know, Mag. I don't want to get caught up in all this stuff."

"Sheila knows how I feel about you. We're working it out. We're both going to therapy. Will you come?"

"Maybe. I'll have to think about it."

"Mike? Don't you ... don't you love me anymore?"

"Yeah. I mean, of course I do. In a lot of ways."

"We need to talk. Sheila leaves at five."

"Okay. I'll meet you tomorrow."

Immediately after Mike hung up, the phone rang again. At the same time, someone knocked on her door. She answered both summonses simultaneously.

"Hello?"

"Come up! I'm making you dinner!"

"Hi, Mike."

Rachel folded her hands in front of her while she waited for Mike to finish talking to Ana.

"What time?" Mike asked. "I have company."

"Oh. One hour?"

"Fine." She hung up, then took the phone off the hook as she let Rachel in.

"We need to talk," Rachel said.

"God. Everybody wants to talk today. I feel like I'm at a convention or something."

"I agree with everything you said at the collective. And I think we should stick together on issues like this."

"That's great," Mike said sarcastically. "Why didn't you say something then instead of waiting till now?"

"I thought you should know first."

"You sat at the bus stop for two hours so you could tell me first?"

Rachel nodded.

"Well, fine. So we'll stick together."

"Great. You want to go to dinner or something?"

104

Mike couldn't help laughing a little at her sudden popularity. "Sorry. I'm not laughing at you. I'm already having dinner."

"Tomorrow?"

"Uh, no. I have to see someone at dinnertime. Maybe after collective next week. We could go out for wings or something."

She gently nudged Rachel out the door. "Thanks for coming. I like being first."

She closed the door and rested her back against it as if guarding against any more intrusions. She needed space. She chuckled again as she remembered how Leslie always seemed to need "space." She needed to rest for work and do laundry and clean her house and write a letter and pay bills and all the things people complain about that keep them somehow sane.

❏ ❏

Monday came faster than Mike wanted it to. She knew it was important for her and Maggie to talk, and she knew she definitely had things she needed to say, but their relationship scared her. In many ways, it was too needy. Mike suspected she used Maggie for a connection to the community, to music, and to gain approval. She loved Maggie, and loved being with her, but she was also afraid to be without her. Mike knew that kind of fear wasn't healthy.

She waited in a parking lot across from Maggie's house until she was certain Sheila was gone. She parked on the edge of the lot so her car faced the house and then reclined her bucket seat so she could just see over the dashboard. The late-afternoon sun caressed her face as she watched people coming home from work and dogs being walked and couples getting to know each other after a long day. The whole scene was peaceful and calming, as if life could really be easy.

"Out of the car, please. Keep your hands where I can see them and get out of the car."

Mike could only see the cop's belt buckle as he stood by her car window and gave his commands. A quick look in her rearview mirror showed the squad car and another cop on the radio calling in her license plate number. Mike carefully opened the door.

"What's wrong, Officer? What did I do?"

"Just turn around and face the car with your hands on the roof."

Mike did as she was told while keeping one eye on Maggie's house.

The cop frisked her and seemed stunned when he realized he was touching breasts.

"Uh, okay, you're clean, ma'am. You can turn around. I need to see your license and registration."

"Would you mind telling me what this is about?"

"Why don't you tell us why you're sitting here?" he asked.

"I'm waiting for a friend to get home. She lives in that house right over there and I'm supposed to meet her."

"Five sixty-four?"

"No. Five sixty-two. The brick one."

He checked her identification and then signaled to his partner that everything was okay.

"Got a complaint from the house next door," he explained. "They said some guy was staring at their house and they were afraid you were gonna burglarize it."

Mike grabbed her ID cards, no longer afraid to show her anger. "Well, I'm not a guy and I don't steal. So, if you don't mind, I'd like to get back into my car and wait for my friend."

She got in and slammed the door, but the cop didn't leave.

After a moment, he leaned down and peered in her window.

"How come you're waiting here?" he asked. "Instead of in her driveway or in front of her house?"

Mike saw Sheila's car pull out into traffic and she started her engine. "I like it here. Or at least I did. Now, if you don't mind, I have to go."

She stared at him until he moved out of the way and then backed up past the squad car. She put her pedal to the floor to squeal her wheels, but quickly thought better of it. She didn't need any trouble right now. The cops watched her pull into Maggie's driveway and kept an eye on her while she waited outside the door. When Maggie finally opened up,

106

Mike quickly put a hand on her shoulder so the cops would see that they knew each other.

"Quick," Mike said. "Put an arm around my shoulder and lead me in."

Maggie didn't ask any questions. As soon as the door was closed, Mike went to the window. The cops slowed in front of the house before driving away.

"Nice neighbors," Mike said as she closed the curtain. She turned to face Maggie and stuffed her hands in her pockets. "Hi."

"Hello." Maggie whispered her usual greeting and inched her way toward Mike. "Are you ... okay?"

"Depends," Mike answered. "We're gonna talk, right?"

"Right."

Mike pushed some books out of the way and sat on a chair away from Maggie who positioned herself on the corner of the couch. After a few moments of tense silence, Maggie geared up for what Mike knew was going to be a dramatic soliloquy.

"It's so hard," Maggie whispered. She took a deep breath and inhaled some asthma spray. "Sheila knows I'm in love with you, but I love her, too. We've been together for ... five years."

Maggie paused to wipe giant tears from her eyes and Mike felt herself softening. She didn't want Maggie to hurt or Sheila to hurt or anyone else to hurt, for that matter. If Maggie and Sheila loved each other, they should work it out and stay together.

"What do you want me to do, Mag? You want me to leave, I'll leave. You wanna stay friends, we'll stay friends. Tell me what you want."

"Make love to me."

Mike shook her head and stared at the floor. "That's not the answer, Mag."

"I want you to make love to me, Mike. Please."

It was a test. If the lovemaking was good, it would somehow make any decisions that had to made a little easier. Mike moved to Maggie's side on the couch but kept a reasonable distance as she dried her tears.

"It'll just make things harder, Mag."

"It'll make things better."

Maggie took Mike's hand and gently rubbed it against her face as Mike softly brushed the tears from her cheeks. Their eyes met and massaged each other, each glance a stroke, each blink a touch. Their breathing quickened in unison as Mike moved her hand around Maggie's body without a touch. She could feel the electricity between them, and Maggie gasped each time Mike's hand came close to a sensitive area.

"We'll make love without touching, Mag. But you'll feel every part of me feeling every part of you."

Mike gazed into Maggie's eyes while she traveled her body. A quick glance at a breast, a smooth ride up a thigh. She came close enough to touch the hair on Maggie's arm, but kept enough distance to let natural energy join them. Around and over, up and down, in and out, she moved her hands, and only when Maggie caught her breath in deep release and pleasure did Mike finally let their lips seal the moment.

"It's something special, isn't it?" Maggie laid her head on Mike's protective arm. "It feels ... special."

"Yeah, it's special." Mike pulled her arm away and made Maggie sit up. "But only until Sheila comes home."

"I know. But it's so ... hard. Maybe if I was sure you'd always stay..."

"I can't be sure anymore. I don't know if I'll ever stay anywhere. When you're sure, the passion goes away. When you're sure, you take the other person for granted. Maybe it's better not to be sure."

"But ... if you're in love with someone you *want* to stay, Mike."

"Maybe that's why you can't leave Sheila."

Maggie put her hand to her mouth as if discovering something for the first time. "Do you think I'm ... in love with Sheila, too?"

"Yup." Mike knew Maggie was trying to get her to say it instead of saying it herself. It was easier that way. It became Mike's discovery instead of Maggie's knowledge. "And Sheila knows that, too."

"Oh, Mike! What are we going to do?"

"Think about it," Mike said, rising to leave. "We'll both think about it and play it by ear."

She gave Maggie a hard kiss good-bye and left her sitting on the couch.

❑ ❑

The next day at work, Mike was plagued by phone calls. Maggie wanted to talk some more, maybe bring over some chicken soup. Cassie thought they could go out for Chinese food, and then for ice cream. Rachel hoped Mike would be free and she wouldn't have to wait until Sunday's collective meeting to talk some more. Ana needed errands run for her because she was sick. Amalia's friends needed rides and she needed attention. Marge wanted to make sure Mike would have time for her when she got to Buffalo. Another woman from the collective was checking to see if Mike was busy for lunch.

Mike tried to bring some order to the chaos while convincing her boss that her personal life wasn't interfering with her work. She called Amalia back and told her she'd give her friends a ride if they helped her run the errands for Ana. Then she called Rachel and told her they could meet for dinner Saturday night and that she'd be bringing her old friend Marge with her because she loved to talk politics and needed the company. Then she called Maggie. She said it would be nice to have some of Maggie's soup, but if she wanted to talk, she'd have to accompany Mike to the airport on Friday to get Marge. The last call was to Adrian, the woman from the college. They agreed to meet for lunch after Mike got done teaching her class on Thursday, but they had to finish by 2 p.m. so Mike could get back to work.

All in all, nonmonogamy didn't seem very hard. As long as Mike could keep everyone basically happy, she wouldn't have to make any commitments and no one would get hurt.

Mike met Adrian for lunch and was surprised by the calmness of their meeting. Adrian was one of those laid-back, easygoing people who would never get ulcers and would probably outlive her children. She was straight, or so it seemed, but Mike could tell Adrian was attracted to her and didn't know what to do about it. They said good-bye easily and made no date, but Mike knew Adrian would be around. It was one of those things you feel and can't explain.

She picked Maggie up a little early on Friday so they could warm up to each other before the airport. Maggie was in a nurturing mood and brought three times as much chicken soup as was necessary. They listened to music in the car, made small talk, held hands, and sipped soup.

"Cassie wants me to take her to the gynecologist," Mike said rather bluntly. She was organizing her schedule and thinking out loud.

"Why? Is she pregnant?"

"I don't think so," Mike answered, not realizing that Maggie was joking.

"Oh, Mike, you're so funny. You sounded just like a husband who found out the rabbit died."

"I guess I'm tired or something. I'm sorry. I don't mean to be so distracted."

"That's okay, honey. You're busy. I understand."

Maggie was being almost too accommodating and it made Mike feel guilty. Maggie leaned her head against Mike's shoulder and Mike automatically flexed to make it strong enough for her.

"So. Are you going to take her?" Maggie asked.

"I guess so. She says she needs the support, so I'll go."

"What's the big deal? It's just a gynecologist. Are you taking her to yours?"

Mike looked at Maggie, dumbfounded.

"I don't have a gynecologist," she said.

"You're kidding."

Mike shook her head.

"Mike! You're almost thirty. Everyone needs a gynecologist. Even butches have parts!"

"No way. No man's ever been inside of me and no man ever will be."

Maggie rubbed the back of Mike's neck while she drove and gave her tiny kisses on the cheek.

"Mike," she said soothingly, "there are women gynecologists, too. Some of them are very good."

"Don't need one," Mike said defensively. "Men make women sick. My parts, as you put it, are just fine."

"I'll give you the number of mine, just in case. You can check her out when you take Cassie."

Maggie wanted to stay in the car while Mike went into the terminal to get Marge. Mike knew she just wanted to make sure she got the front seat, so she didn't object. Marge came out bubbly and yacky and barely noticed Maggie was there. She hopped into the back and immediately leaned forward between the bucket seats so she could be closer to Mike. Mike jerked the car a little with the brake so Marge would fall back, but Marge was determined to keep her position. When they pulled up in front of Maggie's house, Maggie told Mike to wait. She came around to Mike's side of the car and kissed her good-bye.

"Take care of your parts," Maggie said as she waved them off.

"What did she mean?" Marge asked.

Mike smiled. "Nothin'. She's just mothering me today, that's all."

❏ ❏

Marge settled happily into Mike's apartment. She was excited about looking into law school, asking about apartments, and calling old friends. Mike felt uncomfortable about their sleeping arrangements, but Marge insisted that their relationship was platonic and they would be merely sharing the most comfortable sleeping space. Mike finally conceded, but not before declaring she would wear a t-shirt and shorts to bed and then demanding darkness while she changed into them. Marge accepted Mike's shyness without question. She, however, chose to sleep in the nude and had no qualms about undressing in front of Mike.

"I love to talk in bed," Marge said. "It's cozy and friendly and it's just so much easier."

"I used to talk to my cousin in bed for hours when I was a kid." Mike's memory wandered through the darkness as she recalled the natural friendships of childhood. "Sometimes we talked about her boyfriends, or the ones she wished were hers. Sometimes we talked about God." Mike sighed and snuggled into her pillow. "Sometimes we didn't have to talk at all. We just eased into being and enjoyed the understanding silence."

111

"I used to pretend I was my cousin's girlfriend," Marge mused. "We'd kiss each other and pretend we were really making out."

Mike rolled over and propped herself up on one elbow. "So did I! Except I was the boy, of course. We'd make out for hours. And we never told, or at least I didn't tell. It was our special secret."

Marge looked up at Mike and caressed her arm. "It's nice talking to you, Mike. I've been so excited about coming here."

Mike smiled warmly. She liked making people feel good and she needed them to feel comfortable and enjoyed.

"It's been lonely in Washington," Marge said tearfully. "I think I really want to come back here."

She started to cry and Mike naturally held her and comforted her.

"You're here now, with friends. Everything will be okay."

They had never been lovers and probably never would be, but Marge's body nestled into Mike's, and together, they relived the warm compassion of childhood. They awoke at daybreak still cuddled, but not still at ease. The fear of vulnerability coupled with years of pain made them shrink away from caring in the light.

"I'll make coffee," Mike said harshly. "But you have to turn your head until I get my pants on."

They shared breakfast and a crossword puzzle, a walk in the park and some sun. Mike enjoyed the time, but she made a conscious decision not to get involved with Marge. Their backgrounds were too different, and Mike knew their compatibility was only temporary. Marge was a woman used to money and privileges that Mike only dreamed of having. Loving each other, or even pretending to, would only be a waste of time. Still, Mike enjoyed their newness and loved the ego boost she got from Marge's apparent infatuation.

They met Rachel for dinner at Greenfield Street and Mike smiled as each woman moved closer to her and vied for attention. She knew now how men felt when women competed with each other and she understood why it made them feel so powerful. She didn't necessarily like the dynamic. She felt almost forced into being dominant, and she was fearful of letting down her guard.

Mike promised Rachel another dinner on Sunday and retreated to her apartment and less pressure. She and Marge watched a movie on television and Mike found herself unconsciously making love on the couch. It wasn't the kind of lovemaking Mike was used to or wanted. It was detached, mechanical, and unlike anything she had done before.

Mike was relieved when Marge left on Sunday. Over breakfast, she told Ana about her weekend. She wanted Ana to be jealous, to fight for her, but Ana just let her talk and acted uncaring.

She called Cassie and again they went out for ice cream and then she slept until it was time for the collective meeting. The meeting was about self-help and Mike wouldn't let herself stay to be embarrassed by the multispeculum viewing. She caught a smile from Adrian as she passed a note to Rachel and then went home to sleep until it was time for dinner.

"I made dinner here," Rachel said when Mike arrived. "It's not so expensive and it's quieter."

Mike liked the idea. Rachel made her feel at home and dinner at the kitchen table seemed more familial.

"You're not from Buffalo, are you?" Mike asked.

"How can you tell?"

"I don't know. You don't have an accent or anything like that. It's just a city kind of thing, a way of looking at things that's not biased Buffalo or small-town America."

"Long Island. Jewish. Upwardly mobile family. Summer camp for nice Jewish girls and political books for bed partners. Does that take care of the small talk?"

"Not bad," Mike answered with obvious appreciation. "Right to the point and no games."

"Now it's your turn." Rachel smiled as she served Mike's spaghetti.

"I can't answer the way you did. I come from a village that hugs its history and greets strangers with maple trees and shady benches. It sucks in the breezes of Lake Erie and fills the air with the smell of tomatoes and purple grapes. You can sit on a park bench at midnight or walk around the block at dawn, and you never have to remember your key or your neighbor's phone number. The noon whistle blows every day and everyone knows the mailman and the paper-boy."

She twirled her spaghetti against a large spoon and marveled at how Italian it tasted.

"Main Street divides the haves and have-nots and every-one's backyard is larger than a city house."

Mike loved remembering, and her voice mellowed as she traveled the town that harvested her.

"I know every tree, every stone in the creek, every favorite place to park, and every quiet place to sit. In the fall, the streets are ablaze with color, and every leaf is a feeling or a thought or a memory of summer. Then they drop and crumble into brown and we burn them, but only at night when no one can see your tears. The smoke roams over the lawns and the driveways, and the sweet smell of another year fills the air and stings your senses until you're ready for the year to end.

"In the winter, the streetlights turn the snow to dia-monds and the snow stays white for days and days. Sometimes, your footprints follow those of a deer, and sometimes, you can't find a path to follow. And sometimes, when the moon is full and Christmas lights shine from every house, you'd swear that angels were dancing in the field and that nothing, no one, could ever hurt you or make you go away."

"Why don't you go back?"

Mike twirled more spaghetti and didn't answer.

"Mike?"

"Sometimes you can't go back."

Mike's heart began pounding at her chest as the foot-steps of her childhood marched across her memory. She wanted to go back. She wanted to fit in. She ached for the safety of innocence.

"I should go. Back to my apartment, I mean. I'm not very easy to be with when I start remembering things like this."

"I'm easy to be with." Rachel reached across the table for Mike's hand. "I'd like to listen. It sounds like a wonderful place."

Mike pulled her hand away and stood up. "I really should go." She fumbled for her keys and wasn't sure whether to leave her napkin on the table or the chair. Rachel rose with her and again took her hand.

"If you leave now you'll only end up feeling worse." She gently put her arms around Mike and laid Mike's head against her shoulder.

Mike let herself flow into Rachel's kindness, and her heartbeat forced power into her arms. She embraced Rachel with gripping need and allowed her pain to turn to passion. As if loving would erase all her anguish, she pulled Rachel to the floor beneath her and devoured any distance that remained between them. She felt the salt from her tears mingle with the juices in her mouth, and only when she felt her strength return and her dignity restored did she allow Rachel to scream in satisfaction.

The food on the dinner dishes had hardened when Mike covered Rachel with a blanket and went out alone into the night.

❏ ❏

Maggie called Mike bright and early on Monday morning and fired a lot of questions at her. Where was she? Why didn't she call? When would they have time together? After discussing schedules and bickering about commitment, they decided to spend two days a week of "quality" time together. Mike was sure she could handle that. It would give them time to try to trust each other and would still allow Maggie's commitment to Sheila.

Cassie made her appointment at the gynecologist, and Mike fulfilled her promise to take her. The office was like any other: paneled walls, cheap photographs, tattered magazines, and alcohol-tainted air. Luckily, the waiting room was empty, so Mike didn't have to feel so nervous about people mistaking her for a man. She helped Cassie fill out the required forms and squeezed her hand a little for luck.

Female nurses opened and closed doors, and a male doctor poked his head in to say "Hi."

"Are you waiting for someone?" he asked.

"Uh, yeah. She's in there. Getting, you know, examined."

"Hey, man, don't be so nervous. Women go through this all the time. It's a piece of cake!"

Mike buried her face in a magazine to laugh. Being mistaken for a man in a gynecologist's office made her wonder about the future of American medicine.

"Is it okay if we wait for the results?" Cassie asked when she finally came out.

"Sure. What kind of results?"

"You know, diseases or problems or whatever."

"They tell you that right away?"

Cassie nodded.

"You're not worried about something in particular, are ya?"

Cassie's sigh told Mike this was another one of those worries it would take forever to find out about.

"They had trouble getting the speculum in," Cassie said. "The doctor's a real nice woman, but after her son, the other doctor here, came in and whispered something to her, she seemed to become more intent on making sure the examination was very thorough. I don't know if they saw something, you know, like cancer or something."

Mike struggled to be compassionate. She was convinced that most cancers wouldn't exist without heterosexual sex. She wished women would realize that danger before it was too late.

"Glad I don't have to worry about that," Mike said. When Cassie sighed again, Mike gently squeezed her hand. "It'll be okay."

The nurse called Cassie into the doctor's office and motioned for Mike to come, too.

"The nurses don't speak English very well, Mike. I think they're Polish."

"The doctor too?" Mike whispered.

"Yeah. She's Polish too. But she speaks and understands okay."

Mike felt a little funny accompanying Cassie for the doctor's diagnosis, but she was always interested in anything new.

"You are with her, yes?"

Mike shrugged her shoulders. "I brought her here."

116

"Good. Now, she has a slight infection, just yeast for now, but it appears to have been, let's say, hanging around for some time. We are checking now for herpes, because we are not sure from the physical examination just what is causing the problem."

She continued talking to Mike instead of Cassie, making Mike very uncomfortable.

"If it is herpes," she continued, "I would like, if you have the time, for my son to examine you to discover whether or not it has come from you. He sees many people here. Wives, husbands. You would not be his first."

Cassie looked completely confused and Mike felt like she was on *Candid Camera*.

"What do I have to do with it?"

"Well. You are sleeping with her, yes?"

No one had ever asked her a question like that before.

"Just once, sort of," Mike answered sheepishly.

"Aha!" The doctor finally turned her gaze to Cassie. "So then maybe someone else gave you this problem and now, possibly, you are giving it to others."

Mike unconsciously squeezed her legs together. Cassie had never touched her, but they had "played" with each other a little. She didn't know exactly how people got herpes, but she was sure she didn't want it.

The doctor continued. "Well. We will wait a few more minutes for the results and then talk about what to do." Again she looked at Mike. "Do you intend to have relations with each other again?"

Mike didn't know where to look. She half shrugged and didn't want to hurt Cassie's feelings. "I guess so. I don't know. Probably. When she's better, I mean. I mean when this is over."

"Do we need to talk about birth control?"

Finally, Mike realized why the doctor was acting the way she was.

"Girls can't make babies together," she said.

The doctor's face turned red as she scanned Mike's body. "I see. Well. My, my. Anyway, you should have an exam to make sure you're okay. Do you have a gynecologist?"

Mike shook her head.

"Then we will see you here. Uh, a week from Thursday. This is good for you?"

Mike hesitated. "No, I don't think so. I really don't need to..."

"Everybody needs to," the doctor interrupted. "I will see you at seven?"

Mike could only shrug and nod. She'd go through with it, if only to show Cassie she wasn't afraid.

The doctor's son came into the office with Cassie's results. He said something in Polish to his mother and gave Mike the thumbs-up sign. Mike could tell he still thought she was a man.

"Only yeast. That's good. I will give you a prescription and we'll be done with it."

As the doctor followed them out, she took hold of Mike's elbow. "You will be here at seven. Be sure of it."

❏ ❏

Mike called Maggie as soon as she got home.

"Mag, what the hell kind of a doctor did you refer Cassie to? The woman is nuts!"

"Oh, she's wonderful. She's just a sweet little Polish lady from the old East Side and she's very good."

"Oh, yeah, she's great. Now she wants to see me."

Mike could hear Maggie's muffled snicker through the phone. "Well, Mike. We all have to grow up sometime. At least it's a woman. That shouldn't be so bad. Do you want me to go with you?"

"No! Anyway, I think Cassie has to come with me so she can get rechecked for some yeast thing."

"Mike? Are you ... sleeping with her?"

"Not really," Mike answered indignantly. "Are you sleeping with Sheila?"

"Of course I am."

"Then everybody's happy. I'll see you Friday."

❏ ❏

Marge called an hour later to inform Mike that she had definitely decided to move to Buffalo. Then Adrian called to ask Mike if she could be her roommate for a while. She'd just

118

broken up with her boyfriend and didn't have anywhere to stay.

Mike told Marge she could have her apartment because she was planning on asking Tony for one closer to Ana's on the third floor and was sure he'd find one for her. Then she told Adrian that as long as it was temporary, she didn't mind if she lived with her. She had to realize, however, that Mike wasn't home a lot of the time and that she shared her space with Ana and Amalia whenever they needed it. Everyone seemed content with the arrangements.

Adrian moved in quietly and immediately got to know Ana and Amalia. "Adrian looks a little like Leslie," Ana said. "That is why you are attracted to her."

"I'm not attracted to her," Mike answered angrily. "She just needs a place to stay. And I'm sleeping on the couch."

"Mike to the rescue?" Ana asked.

"Yup. And loving every minute of it."

❏ ❏

Her appointment with the gynecologist came sooner than she expected and Mike spent the day at work worrying about the hair on her legs and the fact that her fear of being exposed could very well make her faint.

She rushed home from her computers, double-scrubbed her body, and checked for anything that might make the doctor comment. At least the woman doctor knew about her sexuality. This way, she wouldn't have to go through any more questions or weird looks.

Cassie sat close to her in the front seat, and Mike realized she was trying to be supportive. They weren't really lovers and they didn't really date, but Cassie was fun to be with sometimes. She brought out the child in Mike.

"Do you want me to go in with you?" Cassie asked.

"Absolutely not! It's bad enough as it is without you looking, too."

"I wouldn't look, although I'd like to."

"Ha-ha. Stay put," Mike said.

Two nurses gave Mike a paper gown and pointed to the table where she'd be examined. The stirrups were pulled out and ready. Mike had always noticed them folded on the side of doctor's tables, but she really didn't know how they worked. She put on her gown and crept onto the table. One nurse pointed in a commanding way and Mike immediately jumped to a sitting position. Another nurse gave Mike a gentle push to make her lay back and again Mike obeyed as she desperately tried to keep the gown from riding up and showing anything she didn't want seen.

The first nurse grabbed quickly at the elastic on Mike's underwear. "These off!"

"Oh. Yeah." Mike inched them off while covering herself with a short sheet and then stuck them behind her so no one would see them.

The nurses began tugging at Mike's ankles. "Slide! Slide!" they yelled.

Mike slid to the edge of the table as the first nurse again pushed her back into a prone position. Each nurse grabbed one of Mike's feet and placed it in a stirrup. Mike felt all her modesty, pride, and shame flash before her eyes.

"Open for the doctor, please. He's coming."

"'He'? What do you mean? I'm supposed to get the woman."

They didn't understand. Mike had no time to get out of the stirrups.

"Okay," the male doctor said as he put his gloved hands on Mike's knees. "Let's get down to business."

He looked up at Mike's face with a smile and then did a double take between her face and her exposed body.

"Oh! It's you!"

Mike could only look at the ceiling and pray for speed and total anonymity. The doctor spoke to the nurses in Polish. They all looked at each other in astonishment.

"You have to open your legs now. It won't hurt if you relax your knees and just let it happen."

Mike tried to do as he said so they could get this over with, but her very gay muscles refused to cooperate. Her legs shook violently, making her look like a child who wasn't going to make it to the bathroom.

"Relax and open more, please." The doctor took a quick peek. Both nurses rushed to his side to get their own glimpses.

"We'll need an extra-small," he said to Mike and then repeated it in Polish. The nurses nodded in agreement and Mike watched the ceiling start to spin above her.

"Can I ask if you're a virgin? You're very small."

Mike didn't answer and couldn't have if she'd wanted to. Every bit of her strength was stuck somewhere between her chest and her throat.

"Let's see if you can take a finger first," the doctor said. "You are gay, right?"

Mike closed her eyes and involuntarily tried to keep him out.

"Now, now. Relax. That's better. Yes, you take a finger nicely. This way I can feel for some things inside and make sure there is nothing swollen."

He pulled his finger out. Mike was certain her bladder wasn't going to put up with any more. Before she had a chance to squeeze her knees together again, she felt the ice-cold metal of the speculum.

"Relax more, now. This is a very small one, but it still fits a little tight."

All Mike's resistance was gone.

"That's better. See, it's not so bad. You may even like this a little."

Both nurses again peeked around Mike's knees. That was the final straw.

"That's it, perverts!" She tried to sit up with the speculum still in her and then yanked it from her body so hard it flew from her hand and skidded across the floor.

"Just a minute! You can't do that!"

"Wanna bet, asshole?"

She put on her underwear while she glared at their incredulous looks, and ripped the paper gown away from her chest.

"This isn't right," the doctor said. "It's just a simple exam. There's no need to get so upset."

"How 'bout you getting up on that table?" Mike made a fist and held it under his nose. For a moment she wished she had a gun so she could force him to go through the same indignities. "Go on. Get up there and spread your legs and let me see how you take fingers and weapons!"

The doctor backed away from the table as if afraid Mike might really make him do it.

"Chickenshit," Mike said as she buckled her belt. The nurses cowered in the corner as she put on her shirt. She cupped her hand under her breast and pointed it toward them.

"Does this look different than anyone else's? Does it turn you on? How about you, Doc?" She jiggled it in his face and ogled his crotch. "Does it get you all hot and worked up? Ah, fuck you!"

She stormed into the waiting room and grabbed Cassie by the blouse to drag her out of the office. "Wait a minute, Mike. I'm not done yet."

"You're done! You don't need this crap!"

"What happened? They're nice doctors, or at least they've been nice to me."

Mike let go of Cassie's blouse in disgust and reached into her pocket for money.

"Here," she said, throwing a ten-dollar bill at Cassie. "You like this shit, you stay and enjoy it. I'm getting the fuck outta here. That's your cab fare back home."

She was so angry she could hardly find the handle for the door. When her hand slipped off the second time, she spun around and hoisted a chair over her head.

"Mike! Stop it! What are you doing?"

"Using the only power I have." The chair crashed against the wall and Mike was out of the office before it hit the floor.

❏ ❏

She went home to a clean house: Adrian's way of saying thank you.

"You have messages from the whole world," Adrian said. "Let's see, three from Rachel, one from Ana, and four from Maggie. They all wanted you to call as soon as you got in."

"Great. Have you eaten yet?"

Adrian shook her head.

"Let's order pizza and hide out for a while." Mike took the phone off the hook after she placed her order and instructed Adrian to only keep the back lights of the apartment on so no one would know she was home.

They sat on the floor and ate a quiet pizza in the dark while they talked about the women's movement and families and how smart and cute Amalia was.

"She talks about you like you were a parent or something," Adrian said. "She really adores you."

"We're all parents or something," Mike answered. "And as far as that kid goes, I'd do anything for her."

❏ ❏

By the middle of summer Mike's horrendous schedule of women, coupled with her increased workload at the university, began to carve away at her health. She suffered from migraines, exhaustion, cold sweats, and the inescapable fear of a heart attack. She knew her life had to change quickly, but there never seemed time to figure out how.

Her relationships had all grown in intensity, though none were positive. She and Rachel felt like family. They often left each other notes expressing a closeness that would endure. Of all her relationships, Mike feared theirs the most, because it seemed the easiest. They liked each other, and Rachel somehow knew how to accept Mike's limitations and inability to make a commitment.

Adrian had fallen in love with Mike. She was Mike's calming force. It was to her Mike ran when the anxiety attacks became too frightening or pressures from others too strong. They joked about running away somewhere and leaving everyone else behind. But they also fought, and it was always about men. Mike felt Adrian was too male-identified, too ready to defend anything a man did.

Cassie was the one who hurt the most. She needed Mike's compassion and she needed a patience Mike no longer had. She was young and struggling with a sexuality that threatened her relationship to her family and her music. She needed at a time when Mike could no longer give, and it often resulted in bitter words and destructive attacks.

"I feel like I have to hurt her," Mike told Ana. "If I don't get her mad, she won't go away. If she doesn't go away, she'll keep getting hurt. Sometimes I lie awake thinking of the most awful things I can say to her so she'll hate me instead of love me."

"You need the courage of truth," Ana explained. "Tell her you can't love her. Tell her why, so she can deal with it."

"But I don't know why."

Mike could no longer separate her feelings for anyone. She'd avoid seeing Maggie and then realize it was Cassie she wanted to avoid. She'd lie to Rachel to be with Cassie and then lie to Cassie so she could see Adrian. The only one she didn't lie to was Ana. Their bond was different; their constant bickering, not threatening. Somehow, they knew nothing would ever change the metaphysical tie they relished. When Mike couldn't find solitude or peace with Adrian, she escaped to Ana's. Sometimes, she'd just sit and watch Amalia do her homework. Sometimes she'd rest on Ana's couch. A few times they would make love or just hold each other, but those times always ended when Ana suspected Mike of needing too much of her love.

Maggie held Mike's soul, but the competition with Sheila was too much for Mike to bear. She knew if she truly wanted to she could take Maggie from Sheila and have her all to herself, but she couldn't do it. She hated herself for not having the courage and she hated herself for wanting it. She dreaded making love with Maggie, because she knew it only deepened her pain and resentment. She didn't want their love to become hate.

"If only I knew what I wanted I could stop all this craziness."

Ana instinctively understood Mike's dilemma. "You get something from each one, something different, and you need it. You have to scrape away all the layers of yourself and make peace with the past. When you do that, you'll be able to love without needing and the love will feel natural, from your heart and your soul and your spiritual mind. Not from your brain."

"But how do I stop? How do I end all the hurt I'm causing?"

❑ ❑

She began with Maggie. Because they always shared so much warmth and humor and it was easy for Maggie to detect Mike's coldness.

"We have to make love, Mike. If we don't, I'll know ... it's over."

"I can't, Mag. I just can't. It's not that I don't love you, I do. But I can't be *in* love with you anymore."

"I see." Maggie gathered all her dramatic self and hardened to Mike's pain. "If you leave, you can't come back. You have to know you can never come back."

"Why does it always have to be so final? Other people break up with their lovers and stay friends with them. Why can't we?"

Maggie thought for a moment. When she spoke, Mike so loved listening to her that she almost backed down from her decision to leave.

"I do. I do stay friends with my lovers," Maggie said. "It's true. But I don't ... I don't think I can do that with you. Maybe it's because I love you too much? I don't know. I just don't believe we could do it."

"I thought you were stronger than that, Mag. I didn't think community pressure would ever make you buckle. They destroyed your chance for an album and they're destroying a friendship I cherish."

"I cherish you, too, Mike. I really do."

They looked at each other as warmly as they could, but Mike couldn't give in.

"I have to go, Mag. I'm sorry, I just have to."

She kissed Maggie's hand in remembrance of their beginning, and her lips to seal their good-bye.

❏ ❏

"So, you've begun the shedding of your skin." Ana wasn't surprised when Mike knocked on her door at 4 a.m. "Who was the first? Adrian?"

"No." Mike's sadness took her voice to a new low and the heaviness she felt barely allowed her to speak. "Maggie. She has someone to go to, so it's easier for her. She can cry to Sheila and to her friends, who'll condemn me. She has the most support to survive."

"And will you survive?"

"Yeah. I'll get over it."

"Amalia and I are moving. To a new house a few blocks away."

Ana waited for her statement to sink in. Memories of Chile clouded Mike's mind. She could no longer feel anything in her heart.

"That's good," Mike said dryly. "More space. For both of you. That's good. Good. When?"

"Next month."

"Hmm. That's almost funny. I'm moving next month, too. To the other end of this hallway."

"Oh, good! In the front?"

Mike nodded warily. "The front terrace overlooks the trees and the church. I'll like it there."

"And Adrian? Is she moving with you?"

"No. But she doesn't know it yet. I haven't gotten around to telling her."

"Uh-huh. No time to do the right thing."

"Okay, okay. I'll go tell her now. Okay? Okay. Good night."

❑ ❑

"Is that you, Mike?" Adrian called from the bedroom. "My God, it's five o'clock in the morning!"

Mike peeled her jacket from her body and shuffled over to the couch. Adrian put on her robe to join her.

"You forgot to finish your sentence," Mike said.

"With what? I don't understand."

"You forgot to say, 'Where the hell have you been?'"

"Oh. I stopped asking that weeks ago. Do you want your messages?"

"No. I never want another message as long as I live."

"Well, a couple of them are important. Rachel's really upset, because you were supposed to meet her tonight. She came over here looking for you and she was crying, Mike."

"Did you calm her down?"

"No. We talked for a while and waited for you to show up. It's her birthday, Mike. You were supposed to take her out to dinner, remember?"

"Oh, God. Shit! I forgot all about it."

"That's it, huh? You forgot? We called Cassie and Ana, even Maggie. Maggie said you left at seven."

"Jesus, Mary, and Joseph. You sound like my damn mother. I forgot, okay? I drove around and then I sat at the waterfront listening to tapes. I just forgot." Mike kicked off her sneakers and leaned back against the pillows. "What did Cassie say when you called?"

Adrian shook her head in disgust. "Does it matter? Do you care?"

"No. I guess I don't. She'll get over it."

"She looks up to you, you know. As much as you've hurt her, she's still in love with you."

"Let me ask you something," Mike said, leaning forward. "How come you always talk to me about how other women feel about me? Doesn't it bother you? Don't you ever feel even a tiny bit jealous?"

"I used to. But Rachel and Cassie and I get together and talk a lot. Usually when you're at Ana's or Maggie's. They're friends and I care about them. If you loved them and were good to them I wouldn't mind at all. And I wouldn't be jealous."

Mike put her head in her hand and tried to push away her headache. It didn't make sense to her that they were better dealing with nonmonogamy than she was.

"Are you coming to bed?" Adrian asked. "You've got an hour and you look like you need it."

Adrian opened her hand to Mike and smiled her into the bedroom. She made Mike cuddle into her arms for a change and then soothed her into a deep sleep.

MY SISTER, MY BRIDE

Dear Mike,

We didn't have time to talk when you got in this morning and you were still sleeping when I left for work, so I decided to leave you this note. I think I should move out. It's too hard for me to watch you come and go and I don't know how to give you the space to be alone. I have a prospective roommate and may be able to move by the first of the month. I'm sorry if this hurts you, but I believe it's for the best.

Love,
Adrian

Mike showed the note to Ana as soon as she had read it. "Great, huh? Now I don't have to worry about telling her she can't move with me."

Ana looked at Mike with disgust. "This is how you treat people?" She shook the note in Mike's face. "You read this and say it's great?"

Mike snatched the note from Ana's hand and quickly reread it. "What are you talking about? She says she's moving out and it's her decision."

"I don't even know you anymore. She's hurting! She loves you and it hurts and you act like you have no feeling!"

"I didn't ask her to move in with me, you know. I gave up my space for her and she's giving it back."

"The hero again. You gave. You let. You don't think about what she's given you."

"You make me crazy," Mike said as she headed for the door. "You know I was going to tell her she had to leave. That would have been worse than this, because she would have felt rejected. This way it's her decision."

"When are you going to listen?"

"When are you going to hear me?" Mike slammed the door behind her.

Mike drove to work at breakneck speed. Ana was wrong. She didn't know what it was like living with Adrian and feeling guilty about not being home. She didn't know what it was like to live with someone who had straight friends and defended men. She was wrong. So what if Adrian loved her. She hadn't asked her to fall in love or to wait up for her or to take messages. She hadn't asked for anything.

She made the final turn into the computer center parking lot and screeched to a stop. Her boss, Hank, was waiting for her outside his office. She purposely walked by him without a glance. He followed her like she knew he would, and he stared at her as he always did. When he started playing with his moustache, she knew she was in for a lecture.

"You're late."

Mike didn't answer. She went to the tool chest and pulled out her favorite screwdriver.

"Five times this month. And three sick days."

"I get my work done," she answered as she removed a terminal board. She hated him. She had a degree and seven more years experience. They had both started at the center the same day for the same pay. Now, he made almost twice as much as she did, and he attended classes during working hours so he could get his bachelor's. The inequity made her resent him; his manner made her hate him.

"Next time you're sick, I want a note from the doctor. And the next time you're late, you'll stay late to make up for it."

Mike reached for her screwdriver and thought about throwing it at him. Instead, she stuck it in her back pocket and went into another room to look for a part. When she was sure he was gone, she eased into the chair at her desk and closed her eyes.

She'd miss Adrian. Maybe she was too male-identified and a little bit of a nag, but she was easy to talk to and sometimes nice to sleep with. Maybe Ana was right.

When the phone rang, Mike quickly looked at her watch and realized she had been sleeping for almost an hour.

"Computer Center, Mike Landetti."

"Mike? Marge."

"Oh. Hi."

"Do you think you can give me your apartment? I really like it. I start in Buffalo next month and I really won't have time to look for a place to live. I mean, we could probably live together, but I think it might be a little too crowded, since I have law books and bookshelves and..."

"Yeah."

"Pardon?"

"I said yes. You can probably have my apartment, 'cause I'm moving upstairs. I'll speak to Tony, the super."

"Do you think it'll be okay? I really have to know because I'm pressed for—"

"Yes," Mike interrupted again. "Tony thinks I walk on water. If I ask him, he'll figure something out."

"Great! Uh, by the way, is it expensive?"

"Two hundred and five including."

"Oh. That might be too much for me. Maybe I'll call some other people. When I was up there before I saw a few other places that might be better."

"I'll get him to keep the rent at one eighty-five," Mike insisted. "It's a nice place. You'll like it there."

"Are you sure? Well, if you say so. It's still a little steep, but I'll trust your judgment."

❑ ❑

When Mike got home from work, Rachel was sitting in the hallway outside her door. Mike's walk slowed to a crawl. She had forgotten to call Rachel to apologize. She had forgotten to send flowers or a card. She had forgotten how much Rachel meant to her, and she didn't know how to make it up to her.

She opened her door and took Rachel by the hand to lead her in. They didn't speak. Mike held open her arms and pulled Rachel toward her. Hugging always helped, and there were no words to ease the hurt or bring back yesterday.

After many minutes of just soothing each other, Mike quickly packed a dinner, led Rachel silently to her car, and drove her to Letchworth State Park an hour away. It was almost dusk by the time they arrived and Mike knew the best place to park so they could watch the deer crossing. She pulled onto a grassy path that divided the woods and faced the car toward the gorge. She turned off the engine and reclined her seat, a signal that Rachel should do the same. Silently she spread chicken, apples, two sodas, and choco-late-chip cookies between them and then pulled out a bag of marshmallows.

"For the raccoons," Mike said. She got out of the car and picked a bouquet of fall flowers and presented them to Rachel. "For you."

She closed her door to lean back and wait and almost instantly the deer arrived, to sniff the air, taste the grass, and ogle the two women. They pranced by the hood and sauntered by both sides as Mike and Rachel kept their silent vigil. When it seemed the parade was over, Mike opened a soda and handed it to Rachel.

"Happy birthday."

One tear escaped Rachel's eye. Mike wiped it away and lightly kissed her.

"Almost time for the bandits," she said. She handed Rachel some marshmallows and motioned for her to get out of the car. "Follow me." Her shoes were like moccasins as she noiselessly led Rachel to another clearing.

"You'll see their eyes first," Mike said. "If you kneel down they'll take them from your hand, but keep your hand flat or you might get bitten."

One by one, the masked critters strutted toward dessert. Mike stood back and let Rachel do most of the feeding. When the bandits had had their fill and the sweet food was gone, they retreated back into hiding and Mike took Rachel home.

❑ ❑

"Did you get my note?" Adrian asked when Mike walked in.

Mike nodded as she surveyed Adrian's half-packed boxes. "Are you in a hurry?"

"No. Just bored. And hungry."

"You wanna go out to eat?"

"With who?"

Mike looked at her with a half smile. "With me."

"Oh. That would be new and interesting."

They went to the only gay restaurant in town, and Mike pretended to be as hungry as Adrian. She ordered wine, told Adrian to have anything she wanted, and made sure she was as relaxed as possible so they wouldn't fight. They both ordered enormous desserts, as if ice cream, chocolate sauce, and maraschino cherries could take the place of the companionship they would soon lose.

They giggled and joked and generally had a good time. When they got home, Cassie was waiting by the front door.

"I'll go visit Ana so you two can talk," Adrian said.

Mike had hoped Adrian would stay so Cassie wouldn't launch into one of her sighing acts, and she also hoped Adrian would come back soon so they could just relax. Mike knew she was scowling as she let Cassie in, but she couldn't help herself. Cassie could take the smallest problem and blow it up into a catastrophe. She was the youngest of all the people Mike knew and she had the most to learn.

They sat on opposite sides of the room and Mike waited for some kind of beginning. She had learned not to ask Cassie questions, because it seemed to be the surest way to generate the sighs.

"I want to talk to you about all the criticism you've had of me lately," Cassie said calmly. "I've been thinking about it and I don't think it's fair."

"Which part isn't fair?" asked Mike.

"I don't think any of it is."

Mike looked at her watch. She couldn't believe it was almost midnight. If she didn't get to sleep soon she'd be late for work again. Her headache returned like a punch to her forehead and she gritted her teeth to answer.

"You mean the part about you always dressing down, pretending you're working class, and looking like a leftover hippie? Or the part about always drawing attention to yourself so that I get the same attention drawn to me? Or maybe, maybe it's the part about not sticking with me when I'm obviously being oppressed, like in doctors' offices or when a man spits at me on the street. Is that the part that's not fair?"

"Those things aren't my fault," Cassie cried. "I dress like me, and if that draws attention I can't help it, and I don't know when you're being oppressed. How am I supposed to know?" Her cries turned to sobs, and Mike's compassion replaced her anger. She was right. How was she supposed to know? She came from a middle-class background and a family that gave her every chance to succeed. She was trying to learn about class differences and trying to fit in by dressing her version of working class. And she didn't know what being gay entailed. She hadn't suffered from it, cried through it, bled with it, or buried it.

"I don't know how you're supposed to know," Mike said warmly. She crossed the room so they could be closer. Cassie leaned against her shoulder. "I also don't know if I have what it takes to help you know. Why don't we sleep on it?"

"Here?"

Mike thought about Adrian's reaction and the things Adrian had said the night before. She liked Cassie and would probably feel the same compassion.

"Yeah, here. But we have to sleep. If I show up at work the same way I did today, I'm going to get fired."

Adrian knocked lightly and came in just as Cassie was getting undressed. She said nothing. She gathered her robe, brushed her teeth, and settled in on the couch. Mike couldn't worry about it. She needed to stop her headache and she knew rest would do it. Almost without thinking she went to the couch and kissed Adrian good night, and then did the same to Cassie. Finally, she crawled into her own side of the bed.

❏ ❏

When Marge arrived a few weeks later, Mike was in the worst shape ever. She had helped Ana and Amalia pack and made sure she and Amalia spent special time together. She had helped Adrian pack and was systematically moving her into her new apartment. At the same time she made sure she and Rachel talked or visited a few times a week, and she was gaining weight from all the double and triple dinners and the many times she shared ice cream with Cassie. Cassie helped clean and paint Mike's new apartment, but it was Rachel who claimed the new space by bringing plants, new pillows, and even an extra toothbrush.

Hank complained about all the personal calls Mike received at work and threatened to remove the phone from her desk. Then he added hours to her schedule so he would have more time for his classes and homework. To make matters worse, the economy caused the university to institute a one-year salary freeze.

She bought vitamins for Jackie and spent whatever time she could at the bookstore, and she counseled students from previous classes she had taught who came to visit her and struggled with their sexuality. As if compelled to deny herself freedom, she bound herself to other people's lives and problems. She systematically drained her own energy, causing the slow erosion and destruction of those around her.

Marge demanded almost constant attention and pushed Mike to accompany her to restaurants, bars, and dances. Most of the time, Mike had to decline so she could keep other commitments, but when Marge, Rachel, and Adrian all got together to take her to a coffeehouse where Maggie was performing, she accepted. This way she could see all three and maybe still have time for herself.

Maggie was back at Greenfield Street, and Mike's foursome took a corner table away from the crowd and separate from the community leaders who now labeled Mike a homewrecker and a cheater. When Maggie stood at the microphone and sang Mike's song, all of Mike's buried sorrow and hidden fears and absolute distress over not being accepted by those she called her own rose to the surface and burst from the barriers of her pride. She cried and sobbed openly, oblivious to the stares it caused, unconscious of the women close to her. The beginning of any healing is always a storm, and Maggie's music laid bare all of Mike's wounds and scrubbed them to a rawness Mike could then no longer feel.

When the songs ended, Maggie took her bows and the audience applauded. But it was Mike, and only Mike, who stood and clapped to pay homage to the woman who once had loved her. Maggie barely glanced in Mike's direction. Her inability to acknowledge Mike's respect or presence made Mike slump in bitter exhaustion. People whispered and pointed as Rachel and Adrian draped Mike's arms around their shoulders and helped her to her feet.

"What's going on?" Marge asked. "Is she sick? Mike, what's wrong?"

"She'll be okay," Adrian assured Marge. "I think she's just overtired."

"We'll make her some tea," Rachel said. "And I'll rub your back, okay, Mike?"

Mike shook her head and mumbled a barely audible no.

"Can you walk?" Adrian asked.

Mike pulled her arms from their shoulders and pushed the women away.

"I'll be fine. Just leave me alone."

She stumbled and tripped up the street like a man full of too much wine. Over and over she said, "Leave me alone. I'll be fine. I'll be just fine."

The three women stayed close behind until Mike got to her door. Without a word, Mike closed the door on them and left them listening in the hallway. Safe and alone with doors locked and drapes drawn, Mike stripped the clothes from her slumping body and propped herself up against the bathroom wall facing the mirror. Dark circles ringed her half-open eyes and dried blood crumbled from teeth marks on her lower lip. She opened the medicine cabinet and threw bottles from the shelves as she searched for anything that would take away her pain. Rachel's razor hung inside the cabinet door and Mike flicked her finger against the edge to check its sharpness. She held it up to her face and looked in the mirror as she shaved it across her cheek. Slowly, she let it travel down her neck and across her throat.

"What are you doing, Michaelene?" she said to herself. The razor slid up the other side of her neck and across her cheek. "Is this how you show the world how tough you are? You think this will make you feel better?"

She studied the razor in the mirror and then dropped it into the trashcan next to her.

"Mike?" Rachel called softly through the apartment door. "Are you okay? Do you wanna talk or anything?"

Mike closed her eyes and shook her head as if Rachel could see her.

"Mike? C'mon, Mike. We know you're not sleeping. Can you open the door so we can see you're okay?"

Mike slowly put on her robe, carefully tied it closed, and then opened her door. She kept one foot behind it to block any entrance.

"See? I'm fine. I just need to go to bed."

The three women looked at each other and then back at her.

"You don't want any company?" Rachel asked.

"No. I need to be alone for a while."

Adrian smiled in understanding and Rachel's eyes welled up with water.

"If you need anything, I'm right downstairs," Marge said sweetly.

Mike saw the jealous look on Rachel's face, but she couldn't do anything about it. They'd have to work it out themselves. She motioned for them to leave and then retreated back into the darkness to listen to Maggie's tapes and rid herself of any more tears; but it didn't work. Sometimes, the only way to be free of emotional pain is to give it back to someone else.

Dear Mag,

No one will ever know how deeply I ached for you tonight. I miss you. I miss listening to love songs in the car and telling you stories only femmes can understand. I miss the way you needed me to care for you and the way your hands told me, "Thank you for loving me." I miss your smile and that wonderful laugh that climbs the scales of male and female and sings of

joy without shame. You were as beautiful as ever tonight and I applaud you as I applaud the beauty and
wonder of your music. This is my kiss on your hand.
My tears form the single rose that is only for you.

She delivered the letter to Maggie's door and touched the
wood in a final farewell.

❏ ❏

Mike took the phone off the hook and slept through Saturday
and most of Sunday. She opened the large double doors that
led to the grated terrace and propped pillows on the floor so
she could lie back and watch the trees. It was a hot, sticky
day, the kind that didn't let you breathe, but Mike was
cooled by the sight of green leaves and the veiled blue sky
behind the church steeple. She could dream here. Her other
apartment had been too boxy, too crowded with first-floor
distractions.

She replaced Maggie's tapes with music from the fifties
and sixties and then settled into her new surroundings. The
Everly Brothers sent her back to Sharon; the Supremes
made her remember Leslie. It was okay. She didn't miss
Leslie anymore, at least not as a lover. She wished that they
were still friends, but now realized that some lovers can
never be. She missed Sharon, though she didn't know
exactly what she was missing. They had only spoken four
times since high school and hadn't shared any real time
together since Mike was fourteen. But somehow, Mike felt
they had stayed lovers all that time and something in the
trees always told her that someday they'd love again.

By nightfall, Mike had had her fill of Anka and Dion and
Elvis and all the brothers from the fifties. She felt better. She
wasn't healed, but she knew now that she could make the
changes she needed to and she'd do it honestly.

She called Rachel and asked her to come over and then
called Marge and Cassie and Adrian and told them she was
okay and they shouldn't worry and she was going to spend
some time in her new house and she'd call in a day or two.

When Rachel arrived, Mike could see in her eyes that she
already knew what was going to happen. Remembering one

of Maggie's songs about breakups and letting people down easy, she didn't rush into a hard speech. She offered Rachel tea and a pillow near the terrace. For a while, they just watched the sky turn blacker. It was Rachel who started the process of leaving.

"Can you stay my lover for just a little?" she asked. "Until I'm more ready and won't miss you so much?"

Rachel's tears came quickly and Mike hardly knew how to respond. "I'm not going anywhere," she said.

"Isn't that why you asked me over?"

"Yes. And no. I don't want you out of my life. I just want our relationship to change so it's better for both of us."

"I'm afraid, Mike. Sometimes we act so married, and I love doing things for you, but I'm afraid of loving you."

Mike put her arms around her and kissed her on the forehead. "It's okay. And sometimes it feels good that we act so married. But I'm not ready for that, and I don't want you to think I am."

Rachel wiped her eyes and snuggled into Mike's arms. "This is the first time we've been alone in weeks," Rachel said. "It feels nice."

"I'm surprised Marge hasn't knocked on the door," Mike said. "She's usually checked in two or three times by now."

They held each other tightly and fell asleep in the warm night air. At 5 a.m., Mike sat up quickly and scanned the dark room.

"What's wrong?" Rachel asked.

"I don't know. I just had this feeling. It was so strange. It wasn't a dream or a nightmare, just this feeling that something happened."

"Pisces," Rachel smiled. "You're all psychic."

Mike wiped the sweat from her forehead, then rolled onto her stomach to watch the beginning of morning. Rachel cuddled against her. Mike was glad to see happiness on her face. Maybe they could make things work so they could still be close. She didn't want to marry Rachel, but she also didn't want to lose her.

At 6:30 the phone rang and Mike jumped to answer it.

"What? Where are you? Give me the number again. Oh shit, Marge. I'll be right there."

"Mike?"

"Marge was raped in her apartment," Mike said, dressing quickly. "At five this morning a guy came through her window and raped her. She's down on Crescent at some stranger's house."

Rachel threw on her clothes. "That's what time you woke up, Mike. Right at five."

"I know. I'm also the one who told her to take that apartment."

Mike sped the two blocks to Crescent and searched for a house with the light on. Rachel stayed in the car as Mike knocked on the door. A friendly old man motioned for Mike to come in. Marge was seated on the couch dressed in a man's shirt and nothing else. When she saw Mike, she ran crying into Mike's arms.

"He came in and trapped me! And he stayed and stayed!"

As Mike caressed Marge's head, she squinted to hold back her own tears.

"When he was done he asked where my money was. Somehow I got him to go to the kitchen, and when he left the room I threw myself out the window and ran."

Marge pulled up her shirttails to show Mike the scrapes from the windowsill.

"I ran and ran," she sobbed. "When I got to this street I saw the light on the porch and I pounded on their door until they answered."

The man and his wife looked at Mike sadly. "She didn't want us to call the police until you got here," he said. "Poor thing was stark-naked and shaking to death. We didn't know what else to do. I gave her one of my shirts, but that's all she'd take."

Marge slumped into Mike's arms crying harder. "You're okay now," Mike said. "No one's gonna hurt you now."

She led Marge to the car and thanked the couple for their help.

"Rachel, you have to go to the hospital with her. I'll drop you off and call the police, but then I'm going back to find the son of a bitch who did this."

Rachel agreed. "Make sure you tell the cops you want a policewoman, not a man. And I'll call the rape crisis people.

They'll send someone who'll make sure the hospital does what it's supposed to."

Mike pulled up at the emergency entrance and helped Marge into the examining room. "No male doctors," she said sternly to the nurse. "I don't want another man near her." She brushed back Marge's hair and promised to be back as soon as she could. Rachel nodded to assure Mike she'd take care of things, and Mike raced back to the apartment building.

"Tony! Tony, wake up!" She pounded at Tony's outside door and threw stones at his window. "Tony! It's me!"

"Peter!" Tony stuck his head out the window and looked around. "Peter, what's happenin', man?"

"C'mon, Tony. There's been a rape and I need your keys."

Tony dressed quickly and met Mike outside Marge's open window. Bits and pieces of Marge's life lay scattered and broken on the ground.

"He went this way," Mike pointed. "He left a trail past the garage and out onto Main Street."

"Who, Peter? How'd this happen?"

Mike explained what Marge had told her and continued looking for anything that would lead to the attacker.

"I want that guy, Tony. And I want security on this damn building. Look at this! Anyone can climb through these windows practically unseen. The only people with a bird's-eye view are ... the people from your building."

She stepped back across the courtyard to eye the window that was once hers.

"Tony, did you see anyone in my old apartment from your bedroom window?" She pointed to Tony's second-floor window and again eyed the angle. "That's your window, right? Am I right?"

"Yeah, you're right. I coulda seen right in there if I was lookin'. But we've been sleepin', since before five, so we didn't hear or see nothin'."

"Who said anything about five o'clock, Tony?"

Tony hesitated. "You did, Peter. When you told me what your friend said."

Mike knew she hadn't told him what time the attacker was there, but she wanted to believe him. She thought they were friends.

140

"Did you ever see me walking around my bedroom?"

"No, Peter. No way. Besides, you always kept your shade pulled. That's a fact."

"Too bad Marge didn't do that," she said shrewdly.

"Now with that you're right. She always kept her shade up and her window..." Tony stopped talking as Mike's fists closed in readiness. "It wasn't me, Peter. Yeah, I see her every night. The girl has no shame. But I didn't see anything tonight. Yvonne will tell you, me and her have been asleep."

"Okay, Tony. For now I'll believe you, but if I ever find out you know anything, anything at all about what happened to Marge, I'll kick your ass so hard you'll be eating your balls for breakfast."

The police checked the apartment for signs of struggle and asked questions about Marge's friends and how she dressed and if she went out at night and how many boy-friends she had and did she always sleep with the window open ... Then, they told Mike they'd have to talk to Marge in a few days because it was police procedure and they were sorry it happened and aren't there a lot of rapes lately and some girls ask for it, but they were sure Marge wasn't like that, and they hoped she had a nice day.

Mike brought Marge back to her house. She gave her a key to the apartment so she wouldn't have to go back to the crime scene, and then she called New York to let Marge's family know what had happened. Rachel promised to stay with Marge while Mike went to work.

Mike was more than three hours late for work. Hank was waiting for her in his usual spot. This time, she didn't ignore him.

"A friend in my apartment building was raped this morning and I just brought her back from the hospital."

He didn't say anything. Instead, he followed her to her office where she automatically opened her tool chest and put her favorite screwdriver in her pocket.

"Did he hurt her?" Hank asked, twirling his moustache.

"Rape hurts," Mike answered.

"No, I mean like beat her or stab her or anything like that?"

"No. A few bruises, but she's okay."

"Hmm. Does she dress weird, like she's asking for it or somethin'?"

Mike slumped over the workbench shaking her head. "Why do men always think women dress just for them?"

"Well, you know, some girls ask for it. They wear shorts or tight dresses or tight jeans. You can't blame a man for wanting something that's put in front of him."

"Is that what you think? You think women can't blame men for raping them or beating them or even killing them because the poor bastards can't help it if women are in the world?"

"I think women ask to be raped, yeah. Look at you! You don't walk around showing off your boobs or letting dresses ride up to your thigh. A lot of women dress like sluts and it turns men on. I think they want to get raped, but they don't want to admit it."

Mike pulled the screwdriver from her pocket and threw it so it stuck in the plaster wall just above Hank's ear.

"People like me get raped, too, asshole, and no woman wants it. You're a sorry excuse for a human being and a perfect example of a cock-loving man. One of these days someone's gonna chop off that little thing you pee with and use it for bait in a cesspool."

She yanked the driver from the wall, stuck it back in her pocket, and spit on the floor in front of him as she walked out.

❏ ❏

On the way home, she stopped at Adrian's to tell her about Marge and work, and to ask for help writing a resignation letter.

"Tomorrow I'll be unemployed and poorer than I've ever been," she said, "but I'll be a damn proud dyke who bows to no man."

As Adrian rode home with her to comfort Marge, Mike cautioned her about telling too many people. "You have to protect Marge's pride. A lot of women don't want people to know they've been a victim like this."

When they arrived, Cassie was sitting with Marge and Rachel was asleep in the bedroom. Marge said her two sisters were flying in from New York and her mother would be with her by the end of the week. She asked if they could all stay at Mike's and Mike didn't see how she could say no. She felt responsible somehow. If she hadn't moved, hadn't insisted that Marge take her place, none of this might have happened. No one told her it wasn't her fault; no one said it wasn't her responsibility.

She called Tony and told him she wanted the landlords to know that the tenants wanted more security on the building and she'd like to talk to them about when it was going to be done.

"We got new owners, Peter. They took over two weeks ago. In fact, you should be gettin' a letter from them tellin' ya they're going to raise the rent. I already told 'em about the rape and they're sorry it happened, but it's none of their business."

"It *is* their business," Mike shouted. "They own this place and we pay for the right to live in it. That includes privacy and safety and it's their business to provide it."

"I'll give ya their address, Peter, and you can tell 'em. They ain't gonna listen to me."

To Whom It May Concern:
    The tenants at Main and Jewel Road have orga-
nized a tenants association effective August 20, 1981,
and have listed as their first order of business the demand for proper tenant security on all three buildings
of said premises. Your prompt consideration in this
matter will be greatly appreciated, and the tenants will
be happy to assist you any way they can in accom-
plishing this task.
                            Sincerely,
                            Michaelene Landetti
                            10 Jewel #7B

    ❏ ❏

"I didn't know we had a tenants association here," Marge said.

"We don't. But I'm calling a meeting for tonight and we'll have one by tomorrow."

143

"Buffalo's never had a tenants association, Mike." Rachel had gotten up when she heard Mike yelling on the phone. "We had a whole class about that in Urban Studies. There's never been a tenants association here because all the attorneys and judges own the buildings."

"The Mafia, too," Cassie said. "The ones from Niagara Falls and New York."

Everyone's eyes were on Mike as she folded the letter to mail it to the landlords. Someone had to fight back. Someone had to protect other women from rape and burglary and whatever else might happen.

"Silence helps no one," Mike said thoughtfully. "My father's father came here from Sicily to escape oppression. He built a tiny business in a small town and tried to live his life in peace. After years of scraping and going hungry he sent for his brother to join him and you know what happened? His brother came to him one day and told him he had to pay for protection, that it was the Italian way of doing things. My grandfather loved God and his family and his brother, and he hated any form of violence and all weapons. But he bought a gun and stood guard at his shoemaker's door to wait for the brother he loved to come back. His brother came with two other men and was surprised to see my grandfather holding a gun. In his other hand was a picture of his wife and two of my uncles and my father. My grandfather held that picture close to his heart and pointed the gun at his brother. He said, 'These are my family, my life, and I will die for them and their freedom just as I would have died for you.' My great-uncle left him alone. He told my grandpa to tell no one about their meeting, but my grandfather couldn't keep silent. He went from store to store and house to house urging people to stand up for themselves and their right to safety and life. He told them that they, too, were his family because they struggled like he did and longed for the same things he did. One by one, they joined him. My great-uncle and his friends went away. The two brothers never spoke again."

Mike sealed the letter and Rachel, who always seemed to understand her best, silently took it to the mailbox.

Mike put a flyer under every door and waited outside while people arrived home from work so she could urge them to come to the meeting. At seven o'clock, she headed down to the basement and arranged papers on the washers and dryers. One by one, they filed in: black and white, young and old. Many knew her from her open house at Christmastime; some were just curious strangers she had never seen before.

Tony arrived and announced that he was a representative of the landlords. They had seen the flyers and wanted to know what was being said. Mike quieted everyone and rolled up her sleeves. She told them there had been a rape, but she didn't say who or in what apartment. She told them they had to stick together because this was their home and that they needed to demand better security.

Some were afraid the landlords would retaliate. Others, closer to Mike's age, knew that grassroots organizing was the only way to win. They agreed to Mike's letter as their first demand and then unanimously elected her president.

"I just want to say," she said as she closed the meeting, "that you were all very brave for coming here tonight and each of your neighbors appreciates it. No one of us can fight them alone, but together, we can win."

They applauded her, and she applauded them, but the battle had only begun.

The notices for rent increases arrived the next morning just as Mike was leaving to turn in her resignation. Marge had spent a sleepless night and repeatedly called for Mike to sit with her and comfort her, which Mike did willingly. Over and over, she repeated her story. Over and over, Mike listened.

Mike threw her resignation on Hank's desk and gathered everything that was hers from her office. She gave Hank the finger as she left the only job she knew.

The next few days were hectic. Mike had to keep the momentum going against the landlords while struggling with the unemployment office and the parade of people through her house. On her way back from picking up Marge's sisters, she stopped to copy a hundred flyers and buy food with the last of her money. She called the newspapers and radio stations to tell them what was happening. By the end of the week, all three television stations had picked up the story. Mike studied tenants' rights and housing laws and increased the scope of her complaints to include all the violations she could find. The landlords threatened eviction, but Mike responded with full determination and confidence.

Dear Sirs,
If security is not installed by the end of next week, the Main-Jewel Tenants Association will proceed to hold rents in escrow and request a full inspection by the Housing Authority.

❏ ❏

She held another meeting to explain the next steps that would be taken and to calm people's anxiety about eviction.

"As long as the rents are paid to an escrow account at the bank, and we've paid in good faith, we won't be evicted. The worst that can happen, and I'm not saying it will, is that we'll get eviction notices. We'll go to court, plead our case, and leave it to the judge. If we lose, the escrow account gets paid to the landlords and they are unable to retaliate in any way."

❏ ❏

Marge decided she needed to go to New York and get away from the building, and she left by the end of the week, which finally gave Mike the space she needed to sort out all the things she had to deal with. She barely had enough money in her bank account to pay the rent to escrow, and if she did get unemployment, which wasn't a certainty, it wouldn't come for six more weeks and would be a lot less than she was used to. She hoped to get some money from the university, and she prayed her car wouldn't need fixing and she wouldn't need a doctor until she was able to afford it.

She scanned her possessions in case she ended up having to sell something, but the only thing of value she owned was her car and she could never sell that. It was still her horse, her only means of escape, her only chance for survival. Without it, she couldn't get the jobs she was trained for because computer repair demanded transportation. Nothing else was worth selling. She had worked for almost twenty years and had nothing to show for it. All her money had gone to rent, food, friends, and lovers.

She looked through the want ads, but Buffalo and the economy were no help to those without work, especially dykes. Adrian told her she could work as a waitress, a statement that brought on another of their fights. And when Cassie said she could clean houses, Mike shouted at her with working-class anger. She hated that they didn't understand her dilemma. She was a butch. If she dressed in a waitress's uniform, she'd look like a drag queen. She couldn't be a waitress or a secretary or do any of the traditional female jobs that they seemed willing to do. She had fixed computers for a dozen years, and the only way to continue that was to move, because Buffalo didn't house any company's headquarters. She wasn't ready for that, either. Moving took money. No company paid to move people anymore. Her anger at Adrian's and Cassie's inability to understand her position increased until she couldn't talk to them. She was no longer afraid of hurting them with her words.

She told Cassie not to come back. She had too much growing up to do, too little class consciousness. When Cassie began to cry, Mike was heartless.

"Go find someone else to put up with you," she said. "You think all your little problems are important, like the end of the world is coming. They're not important, and you're no longer important to me!"

She knew she had said the final words to their relationship. It hurt. She hated to be the attacker. In many ways, she liked Cassie, but she felt she had no choice. Cassie would keep coming back if she was nice to her and their destructive ways with each other had to stop.

The distance between Mike's and Adrian's houses made their breakup a little easier. Adrian didn't drive and seldom took the bus. Mike could put her off by saying she was busy with tenants' stuff and unable to get away.

Rachel was the hardest. Mike still didn't know how to stop the way they related to each other, so she went to the best counselor she had.

"I can't say these things to you anymore, Mike. By now you should know what to do."

"Let me guess," Mike said to Ana. "I should just tell her that I want to be friends and that I don't want to be in a relationship anymore and that's it."

"Right. Finally, you've got it."

"She'll freak out. I know she'll go crazy on me, and I won't be able to deal with it."

"Aha! So now it comes out! It's not her you're worried about, but you!"

Mike hadn't realized what she'd said. She did worry about Rachel's reaction, because she cared about her and enjoyed her, but the real problem was whether Mike could handle her reaction. If Rachel cried, she'd comfort her. If Rachel got mad, she'd compromise. If Rachel hated her, she'd make her love her again.

"You heard it this time, didn't you?" Ana smiled. "We have a breakthrough here! Amalia? Come in and give Mike a hug!"

"You don't have to gloat," Mike said. "This doesn't really solve anything."

Amalia jumped onto Mike's lap and almost knocked her over. "Geez, kid, you're getting heavy. You must be growing up."

Ana laughed out loud. "So are you, chiquitita. So are you."

"C'mon, kid. I'll take you out for a burger."

"Am I invited?" Ana asked.

"Only if you stop laughing."

"Yeah," Amalia chimed in. "No laughing. Growing up isn't funny, right, Mike?"

"Right."

❏ ❏

Mike asked Tony to find Marge a new apartment on the third floor and wrote a letter to the landlords expecting them to comply with previous demands and not to block Tony's efforts to give Marge security. The apartment was ready by the time Marge returned from New York, and Mike moved all of her things upstairs for her.

Daylight saving time went away and Mike pressed harder for compliance from the landlords. She registered multiple complaints with the Housing Authority, finally forcing them to send over a building inspector. When one of the landlords showed up with him, Mike decided that she would accompany the inspector, too.

"Who are you?" the landlord asked.

"Landetti from 7B."

"Oh, it's you. Get lost. This is a private inspection."

"Sorry, you're wrong. I have a right to accompany the inspector because I rent space on these premises."

Though they kept her from entering anyone else's apartment, she followed them and took notes on everything they saw.

"Paying your rent today, Landetti?" the landlord asked loudly.

"Right into the escrow account like everyone else."

"You know, you're the only problem we have around here. If you were gone, things would be nice and peaceful." He threatened her with his stance, but she didn't back down.

"And if you and your buddies were gone, things would be peaceful and safe," she said.

The television cameras were waiting for her when the inspection was over, and after the interview, Mike decided she'd better call home and tell her parents why they were seeing so much of her on TV. She'd also take the opportunity to let them know she was unemployed. Maybe make them guilty enough to want to help her out financially. After all, they were parents, and though they hardly knew her, she did see them once in a while and she was in a little trouble.

"Hi, Dad."

"We've seen," he said immediately. "Is it worth it?"

"I think so."

"Why don't you just move?"

"Why should we have to?"

"Do you want to talk to your mother?"

"Only if she wants to talk to me. I just called to let you know what was happening. By the way, I also lost my job."

His silence told her that this was something he cared about. "Any prospects?" he finally asked.

"Nope. No unemployment yet either."

"Well, get out there and look. Here's your mother."

"You know you're drawing a lot of attention to the family again, Michaelene. Some people don't agree with you and it's not good for your father's business. My salon customers don't want to hear it either."

She heard her father telling her mother not to talk about it, but her mother insisted.

"It would be nice if you thought about us for a change instead of sticking your neck out for a bunch of strangers."

"They're not strangers. And I live here, too. What do you want me to do: just forget about the rape and the lack of security? What if it was me who was raped?"

"That's different. It isn't you. Why doesn't she fight for herself?"

"Because I am. I have to go."

"Wait. Your father has something to say."

"Mike? I'll keep my ears open for jobs for you. Maybe something will open up down here, away from the city."

They said their good-byes and Mike knew it would be Thanksgiving before they spoke again.

❑ ❑

Between fights with the landlords, tenant meetings, and job hunting, Mike visited Ana, spoke to housing lawyers, and hung out at the bookstore, especially when Jackie was there.

"That nice woman always takes good care of me," she once told a co-worker.

Marge and Cassie started sleeping together "as buddies," they said, and Mike could see that Cassie hated her with every bit of her heart and soul.

"She says she's a fool for ever caring about you," Marge told her.

"She won't always think that," Mike replied. "She has to hate me right now, and maybe she will for years. I don't want her to, but I can't stop it. Hopefully, someday she'll see me as an experience or something that was necessary so she could move on to other things."

"Rachel's not doing very well, either. She says you never call to see if she's okay."

"She's right. And she's also tough." Mike felt a forgotten sadness start to well up inside of her, and she fought to keep it away. "She'll probably hate me longer than Cassie does, maybe forever. She holds her feelings deep inside of her and they'll take longer to surface."

"You sound like you still love her."

"Maybe," Mike said softly. "She was good to me. I just couldn't marry her."

"You can't marry anybody," Marge said.

After they hung up, Mike knew that Marge, like Cassie and Rachel, would never call again.

❑ ❑

Adrian announced that she had fallen in love with another woman and Mike was relieved. She had somehow known that Adrian would be the one to find peace first. She felt a tinge of jealousy and she recognized the sorrow that she would forever carry with her, but she had stopped hurting people and it slowed the bleeding from her own wounds.

❑ ❑

By the beginning of November, almost every tenant in the complex was attending regular meetings. Mike set up special committees and ran another election so each building could have representatives and other people could start picking up some of the work and fighting for themselves. The landlords did everything they could to divide and conquer: they painted the outside of all the buildings, planted flowers, and replaced locks, but they didn't provide window security, fix leaks, repair plumbing, install outside lights, or do any of the things that would comply with tenant demands. They threatened to take everyone to court and that frightened many of the elderly, so Mike hired an attorney to speak to them about their rights and increase her credibility.

Tenants knocked on her door day and night to tell her of new threats or speak about strategies or just to feel more secure. She opened her house for Thanksgiving and called Fredonia to tell them she was looking for work and too tired to come home. People filled her house, but Mike felt an emptiness in her heart.

Ana and Amalia were still only a few blocks away, but Mike never seemed to have enough time to visit them. She still walked to the bookstore every morning, but the only time she felt good about being there was when Jackie was working. Jackie made her feel good. Jackie somehow made her feel stronger.

The snow began in early December, and rent money continued to go into escrow. One landlord wore a gun on his ankle and told Mike bad things can happen to people who cause trouble. An unknown driver rammed into Mike's car and witnesses said it seemed intentional, because he rammed it three times and took off. She borrowed money to have it fixed and stopped buying vitamins to repay the loan. Her mailbox was pried open and the heat to her apartment suddenly stopped working, but she continued her fight and kept the respect of the tenants she was protecting.

A woman from the second floor came to her in the night and asked her if she needed any help getting newsletters out or planning meetings. Mike was grateful for the offer and the company. She and Linda became instant friends, spending hours discussing every bad thing that could happen and poking fun at the men who thought themselves so powerful.

"The landlords don't like my cats," Linda said. "So I hide them or let them out through the windows whenever they're around the building. The man I live with doesn't like cats, either."

"I like cats." Mike told her about the eight cats and two dogs she'd once had and how a roommate went crazy one day and let them go. "The neighbors said my roommmate killed them, but I searched the West Side for weeks and finally found one with a bell around its neck. It didn't recognize me anymore and I figured she had a good home, so I left her alone."

"Was your roommate a man?"

"Nope."

"I thought not." Linda smiled seductively, and Mike knew she was in trouble. "When I saw those arms at the first meeting, I had a feeling about you."

"Does it bother you?"

"Hell, no! I'm just with this man because, for a while, it was convenient. He's kind of like a sugar daddy. But I don't

152

like labels, so I don't tell people I'm straight or gay or anything. I'm just me. When I fall in love, I just do."

At the next meeting, Mike purposefully rolled up her sleeves to get a reaction from Linda and she caught herself flirting with her whenever Linda allowed it.

When the tenants planned a Christmas party, Mike taught them how to share the workload by making it a potluck. She couldn't give Christmas to anyone else. There was barely enough money for a gift for Amalia and there wasn't enough to buy a tree. Unemployment wouldn't start until January, and then it would only be enough to just get by. She had no gas to drive to Fredonia, no quarters to buy strangers coffee. This year, the strangers who called her friend would give her Christmas.

There was music and wine and too many desserts, but even the elderly got into dancing a little and having a good time. Mike drank a little more than she was used to and danced with everyone who asked. Most of the men kept their distance, but a few were into dancing with anyone, so she didn't reject them when they asked. Linda didn't dance, but Mike noticed her watching her every move and it excited her that she was interested. By the time the party was over, she and Linda were pretty drunk and Mike knew when Linda staggered up to the third floor with her that they would end up in bed.

"You're one of the most beautiful women I've ever seen," Mike said, pressing Linda against the wall. "I can't stop looking at you. Ever since you walked into my house I haven't been able to take my eyes off you."

Linda was a little nervous, but she was a tough Italian from New Jersey and closer to Mike's age, so she didn't show any fear or back away from something new.

"What planet are you from?" she asked.

"Venus."

"I believe it. I've never known anyone like you."

"Maybe you should get to know me better," Mike whispered. She pressed her body against Linda's and teased her by slowly kissing her neck. She let her kisses travel slowly up to Linda's ear and she made sure her breath was hot so Linda could feel the breezes of her passion. She gave her only

153

a light kiss on the lips to test her response and then traveled down her other side to nibble on her left shoulder.

"If you want to make love to me, let's do it," Linda said as she wrapped her arms around Mike's neck. "I want to make sure you're going to follow through and not just stand here driving me crazy."

Though they were the same height, Linda was built much smaller than Mike, so it was easy to lift her and carry her to the bedroom. There was no ritual, no slow acceptance, no modesty. Their passion ripped through them as they tore the clothes from their bodies and scrambled into each other's arms. Linda fell on her back and pulled Mike down on top of her. They kissed hard and deep, letting their hands go up and down and under and into all the flesh, the curves, the tiny crevices that separated them and kept them from becoming totally one.

"Fuck me, lick me, eat me, do anything you want," Linda panted. "I've never wanted anyone so badly in my life. I want to suck you inside me, feel all of you." She pulled at Mike's legs, grabbed first one breast and then the other and stuck it in her mouth.

Mike fluttered her tongue on one nipple and then the other, sucking, licking, teasing the tip until Linda couldn't push her breast any closer. She moved her hands lightly up and down Linda's body, grabbed her fleshy thighs hard and kneaded them, then let her fingertips drag softly up the inside to curl into Linda's hair. Her tongue tracked down Linda's beautiful body, across her belly, into her navel, and around, down the outside of her leg, and slowly up the inside, curling, licking, sucking in her flesh.

Over and over they came into each other's arms until their thirst was quenched, their need replaced with total depletion.

Like children caught in a lie, they covered themselves and lowered their eyes as the winter sun melted through the icy window. "Don't fall in love with me," Mike said as she stole a puff of Linda's cigarette. "And, please, don't let me fall in love with you."

"I won't. But we can have some fun for a while, can't we? I have to tell you, that was really something."

154

Mike felt proud. She had worried that her lovemaking skills would shrivel with her past relationships, and she had kept herself from testing them, because she feared expectations. Linda wasn't gay, but she was the kind of femme every butch needs as a friend. They'd be lovers when they had to, sisters when they needed to, and friends because they wanted to. They didn't need to talk politics, because their backgrounds gave them all the theory they needed to survive. They didn't fight about money, because they both knew money was to spend or lose or never have. It was the first time in Mike's life that she had a woman she could love just as a friend, and she relished it. But she also feared community pressures. She didn't want Linda stolen away, destroyed by gossip, or caught up in some clique that would forever make her hard. So she kept her hidden, a name with no face, and shared her only with Ana and those who already knew her.

Ana liked Linda immediately and Mike knew she was studying their relationship. Suddenly Ana changed. Mike felt Ana's jealousy through her bitter words and her kisses. Ana came to her for more touches, hugged her more often, teased her into lovemaking, and showed her how well she could love. She wanted Mike to treat her the same way she treated Linda, but Mike couldn't. Her feelings for Linda were almost superficial, and she knew Linda couldn't hurt her. She loved her, but not in a way she had ever loved before. Her love for Ana was too deep to play the same kind of game. She could never only love her for a while or only love her for fun, and she didn't want Ana to play with her heart, so she visited less often and talked much less. She created a distance that would hurt and that she knew would last. She'd always be there when Ana needed her, and she'd always be what Amalia needed her to be. She couldn't, however, be a toy, and so she couldn't be Ana's lover.

❏ ❏

Linda's roommate moved right after the new year began, and she and Mike became constant companions. They shared dinners and books to cut down on expenses and often cuddled at night to keep away the cold.

"I'm going to have to find a different place to live, Mike. The cats keep sneaking out and the rent's too steep." She paused and lit a cigarette. "Do you think we could handle living together?"

Mike smiled and looked down thoughtfully. "No. I have too many dreams. I want to make enough money to live in a nice place with someone I'm going to spend the rest of my life with. Be married to her through thick and thin. Besides, I can't move while all this tenant stuff is going on. That's just what the landlords want me to do."

"Hmm. Well, I have to go, with you or without. I'll move close, so we can keep in touch. Maybe you could stay over once in a while, you know, talk through the night or just be around? We'll keep it like old times. Getting home from work after midnight is pretty bad when there's no one around. I don't know how I would have done it without you."

"That all might change anyway. I have an interview to be a counselor at an employment agency. Me, the one lookin' for work. I'm going to show other people how easy it is to find a job. Anyway, that's nine-to-five with homework, so I wouldn't be able to stay up all night anymore."

They looked at each other simultaneously, as if realizing for the first time that a change was coming they weren't ready for.

"Wanna play around as a kind of good-bye?" Linda snuffed out her cigarette and looked at Mike coyly.

"I'll play," Mike said, "but it's not good-bye."

❏ ❏

Mike convinced the head of the employment agency that she could do anything she put her mind to and he told her she could start March 15. She borrowed money from Linda to get clothes suitable for downtown business, yet butch enough to keep her comfortable. She had a few dollars left over, so she went to the health food store to buy some E's and C's to give to Jackie. She didn't know why, but Jackie was the first person she wanted to tell about the job and the first one she wanted to see. She brought her the vitamins and a lot of literature, her excuse for staying longer than just a delivery would allow. They sat at her kitchen table and talked very clinically about Jackie's cyst and what she had done to treat it so far, and how many vitamins to take to heal it. When Jackie offered to pay for the bottles, Mike seized the opportunity to let her know how she felt.

"You're my favorite person," she said, and she was shocked by her own shyness. "You always took care of me at the bookstore and never judged me." She hesitated for a reaction, but Jackie only smiled. "You have no idea," Mike continued, "how important your smile has been to me. You have the kind of smile that melts statues."

When Jackie flashed her smile again and turned a little red, Mike knew she was making progress, but then she got stupid, like a schoolboy at a dance.

"It reminds me of Mary Tyler Moore. You know, the way she smiles makes everybody love her? Well, I don't mean everybody loves you. I mean, I don't love you. I like you, that's obvious. I guess it's obvious. Does anyone else buy you vitamins? No, huh?"

Mike fumbled with the bottles until she dropped one and rolled it across the table. Of course, when she tried to react quickly enough to catch it, she jumped up too fast and her knee almost tipped the table over. It hurt so much she spun around to rub it and hit her chair, which made her fall back against the table and knock over the other bottle ... Jackie laughed like any schoolgirl, but was sophisticated enough to try to hide it.

"What a jerk, huh?" Mike rubbed her knee and calmly retrieved the bottles while Jackie steadied the table legs.

"You have to answer a question like that," Mike said. "When someone like me calls herself a jerk and acts like I just did, you're supposed to say 'Yes' or smile sweetly and say, 'I don't think so.' Got it?"

"I don't think so."

"Ha! You don't think I'm a jerk, or you don't get it?"

"I think it was very nice of you to buy me vitamins."

At that moment, Mike knew that she had loved Jackie forever. They weren't kids, and Jackie wasn't playing games, and though Jackie didn't know it, Mike knew she was the woman she had been waiting for. She was everyone wrapped up into one beautiful package; she had Sharon's softness and Sue's sophistication and Leslie's way of following through and Ana's sensitivity. But her way was uniquely hers, formed by a history Mike ached to hear.

She stayed as long as Jackie would allow and asked her questions about her work, her family, her past. Jackie's eyes showed her pain, and her smile changed as she told of being a mother and a battered wife and losing her children.

Mike felt as if she had suddenly grown two hearts: one filled with love, the other overflowing with compassion. She wanted to hold her and protect her and race through her past to make all the pain go away. She wanted to feel her and soothe her and make her know someone loved her and would never hurt her. But she couldn't move. Her intensity and her fear that this would be the one woman who would reject her made her freeze, unable to speak. She was afraid to move, afraid to reach out, afraid that if she touched Jackie she would crumble into dust, and afraid that if Jackie touched her she'd turn into stone. She could barely watch Jackie's eyes, because she wanted so much to be reflected in them, and she couldn't watch Jackie's hands, because she wanted them around her and she ached to fill them with treasures and memories and rainbows and anything else Mike could find that was beautiful and pure and good. If there was a God, Mike was sure he had sent Jackie into her life and that she was special and needed special love.

Jackie's eyes filled with tears as she spoke of the children she so adored whom she had to leave behind. Every bit of Mike that had ever parented screamed out in pain and understanding, and she silently asked any forces who would listen to please let Jackie's kids come back to her.

She wished they had always been lovers so she could comfort Jackie's memories. She wished they were lovers now so Jackie could begin to heal. She wanted to cry out, "I love you! I've loved you for years and forever!" But she could only clench her fists in anger that another had loved Jackie first and hurt her and caused an anguish Mike was sure would stay. She knew what it meant. She knew Jackie hadn't even begun to heal and that all her anger and misery would someday be directed at anyone who dared to receive it. She knew healing was a storm, as her own tempest was still with her. But the power she felt between them, the incredible, terrifying power she knew would pull them together like thunder and lightning, crashed even now inside her heart and she couldn't turn back.

Her mind raced through loose ends and unfinished business. She couldn't let her love show now, but how could she not? Her heart screamed, "Wait! Wait for me to finish whatever it is I'm supposed to do. Wait for me to be all that I've ever been when I was strong and good and trusted love, so I can be all that you need, all that you'll ever want." If she loved her now, she'd bruise her with her own battered heart and empty her with her need. If she loved her now, the winds of change would pull them into its fury and shred them before their souls could merge, before their hearts could breathe, before they could truly believe that one was made for the other and that love can last and grow and struggle and survive.

But if she turned away, where would love go? What time would ever come again when tears needed to be answered? What time when the rolling thunder could once again meet the piercing lightning and cause the rain and the quake of their souls to cling together for love's sake?

Mike's heart roared in utter anguish as she struggled for an answer. Jackie ended her story and silently, majestically, waited for Mike's truth.

Mike looked at her with every ounce of life she could draw, with every flower she had ever seen, and her voice became the calm of a forest after a spring rain.

"I love you. And I want to hold you. But only for a moment, only for as long as it takes you to know that I'm here, only for as long as it takes for you to know I'll come back. I won't let go, and I'll go no further, until it's right."

No force could hold them back, no strength could pull them closer. Fear stood between them and shared their embrace, and only when Mike felt the beat of Jackie's heart blend with her own did she dare to let go.

HOME

Dear Mom and Dad,

Please read what I'm about to say with all the understanding you can find, and don't be afraid. I'm not writing to tell you I'm sick or dying or to tell you any secrets you don't already know. I'm writing to both of you and to each of you because it has to be done, because we have to fix whatever it is that got broken years ago.

I'm a woman who loves women, and I'm also your little girl. I'm the baby you held and loved, the child who made you mad enough to beat her, and the teenager who lived away from home. I'm the Marine you could have been proud of, the graduate who finally got all A's, the worker who always does her best, and the friend who loves my neighbor.

You're my mother who nursed me, my father who bounced me on your knee, and the blood that runs through me and bleeds so red is your blood.

Like you, I was born in love with the world. I judged no one, hated no one, marveled at each day, and loved both man and woman. I learned to walk because my tiny hand was in yours. I learned to talk because I smiled at the lips that talked to me. Your thoughts were my thoughts, your laughs were my giggles, and all the pain you ever felt I shared when you wouldn't hold me.

Life got harder for you, but I didn't know. I lived for the sun and the trees and the smiles of friends while you used all your skills to survive. When the days were too long, the work too hard, the money not enough, I still didn't know. I greeted you with childish things, a five-year-old's kisses, an eight-year-old's pranks, a teenager's need to know who she is. But you lived as adults with a past I never shared, and the kisses stung, the pranks were too naughty, and you couldn't know the teenager who shared your home.

I'll be thirty-two on the 20th and I've lived and loved. Sometimes I still give a child's kisses; sometimes I enjoy little pranks; and even now I have questions of who I really am. But one thing has never changed, in spite of our distance, in spite of our pain. I'm still your little girl.

If you need me to be sorry for being too naughty or staying up too late, or for not eating all my dinner or taking out the garbage, or for not staying clean when the laundry was just done, then I can say that I'm sorry.

But if you need me to be sorry for being who I am, for loving when I didn't think I could, for giving when I had nothing left to give, for sharing when all I had was my heart, then please think again. If I apologized for that, I'd be sorry for being your daughter and having your blood and listening to your words and watching your life and being me, your daughter.

I'll never be a princess, and you won't see me in dresses, and I'll never have a husband or share children with a man. But I'll love just as hard, smile just as wide, dance just as long, and parent just as well. If your real wish before I was born was that I be healthy and strong and live a long, happy life, then I'm almost all you've ever wanted, and I'm still your little girl.

Mike sealed the letter carefully and dropped it in the mailbox on the way to her new job.

"These are for you," her new boss said. He placed the bouquet in her hands and stood back with his hands on his hips.

Mike was surprised and very embarrassed. "Thanks, Roger. I never got flowers from a boss before."

"From me? Oh, no. They're not from me. I thought maybe they were from your boyfriend or something."

"Oh. Well, guess I'd better get to work."

She waited until she was safely in her office before opening the card.

Mike,
     Everyone deserves flowers. Good luck with your
new job, and thanks for the vitamins. Love, Jackie.

Mike knew her ears were beet red, but her smile was the truest it had been in years. No one had ever sent her flowers — butches just didn't get them — but she loved them anyway and had a sudden rush of respect for the one who had sent them.

She knew Jackie worked at a bank somewhere downtown, and she roamed Main Street on her lunch hour to see if she could find her.

She wasn't eating yogurt, or hot dogs on the corner, or reading a book in Cathedral Park, or sipping a soda on the steps of the library. Mike looked everywhere she could until she ran out of time. She had to walk fast to get back to her office and she didn't feel as happy as she had in the morning, but she hummed "Dream, Dream, Dream" in the elevator and felt better by the time she got to her desk.

The job was easy, especially for Mike. She somehow knew how to sort out people's strengths and organize their resumes. She was good at helping people be themselves and teaching them to project their talents. Mike felt right at home and glad that her workdays would now end right at five, a schedule she had never enjoyed before.

She rushed home to change her clothes, made flyers for another meeting, called Linda to tell her about her day, and raced to Jackie's to wait for her to come home. From the hood of her car, Mike watched every step Jackie took once she got off the bus. She enjoyed every minute of it. Jackie's legs were meant for nylon commercials, and her walk was smooth, fast, but mellow. When she saw Mike, she smiled her smile for the entire block and Mike knew all was right with the world.

"I sold the flowers and got enough money to take you out to dinner," Mike said, checking the change in her hand. She looked up at Jackie with the smallest smile she could and then rechecked the nickels she'd just counted. "Are ya hungry?"

"I could eat. Sure. Any place in particular?"

"The choice is yours," Mike said. "After all, they were your flowers."

"Can we walk?"

"Whatever you want."

They didn't know yet how to be with each other, and Mike was sure that people could tell she was trying hard to make them look like a couple. She tried walking in step or making sure their shoulders touched and once or twice she thought she touched Jackie's arm as they crossed a street. She looked right and left for people she knew so she could stick out her chest and wave, and she watched her feet a lot so she could listen better and dream a little.

"I was thinking about going to the country this weekend to see if spring is here yet, "Mike said. "You can't always tell in the city, you know? I thought maybe you'd like to go, since you don't have a car."

"Sounds great! But I'll have to think about it."

Mike wasn't put off by Jackie's reluctance. "Ever seen the swamp where the ducks come back to nest?"

Jackie shook her head, wide-eyed and interested as she daintily ate her Greek salad.

"Ever poked a maple tree when the sap's ready to run?"

Again Jackie shook her head.

"Why don't you say yes and we'll go on Saturday?"

Jackie searched Mike's eyes for trust and safety, and Mike felt that roller-coaster feeling when your heart slides up your chest and reaches out then falls all the way to the pit of your stomach and bounces back to make you catch your breath. She wanted to say, "Trust me. If you'll love me and forgive me and grow with me and know me, I'll never hurt you."

Instead, she said, "I didn't really sell the flowers."

And Jackie replied, "Then I'll go."

❏

Mike's mind wandered at the tenants' meeting and Linda passed her a note telling her people were nervous and needed reassurance, but Mike couldn't keep her heart glued to their problems.

"If you're a leader, act like one," Linda scolded later. "I can tell there's a woman in your life, Lord knows I've seen that look before, but that's no reason to let people down. She'll wait, these people won't."

"Okay," Mike said halfheartedly. "It won't happen again."

Linda lit a cigarette and eyed Mike through stinging eyes. "So, who is this new flame?"

Mike laughed a little at Linda's choice of words but kept her silence as she always did when asked about anyone.

"Uh-oh. Afraid to tell me, huh? It's either serious or you're ashamed to say. Which is it?"

Mike wanted to tell, maybe even shout it from the roof of the building, but if Linda wanted to know about Jackie, she'd have to find out another way.

"Okay," Linda threatened. "I'll ask Ana. If anyone knows, she does. And don't forget! Keep your mind on business. There's a lot of old ladies counting on you." She gave Mike a full-lipped kiss and sauntered away.

Within an hour, Ana was on the phone asking questions.

"So, chiquitita, tell me. I thought you were cleaning house of all these women. I know what Linda is to you, but who is this new one, this flame?"

"She's not a flame," Mike answered defensively.

"Ah! I hear something new in your voice. How serious can it be?"

"As serious as *we* could have been, but better," Mike said.

"Hmm. I think by your tone it is as serious, but don't say better, little Mike. No one else will go through what's ahead for you and still love you."

"You don't love me," Mike whispered after a moment. "If you did, you would have given up your toys or fought for me, but it turned out to be okay. This woman will follow me through anything, and I'll follow her, and the difference will be that we'll love each other while we heal."

"I did, too. You just didn't see."

"No, it's not that I didn't see. I saw you go to a man for comfort, not to me. You loved me so much that you were afraid I couldn't handle your changes, couldn't bear your anger or your pain. I would have. Even if I got angry back or went a little crazy or whatever had to happen, I would have stayed by you through it all."

"How could I know that? I've been crazy with all the things I've been doing to deal with my life. How could I have known?"

"I don't know," Mike answered thoughtfully. "But if you had turned to me, my arms would have held you when you needed them most. Maybe we would have spent one quiet moment holding hands. I don't know. It doesn't matter now."

Mike didn't want any pain to cloud her new beginning. She wished Ana would just quit and hang up, but the silence was long.

"This is serious," Ana finally said. "Protect yourself. There are parts of you not many will know or understand."

Mike said a silent good-bye and pulled the silver necklace from her throat.

Saturday took forever to arrive and Mike greeted her special day by peeking through the shades. "Hello, sunshine! Hello, spring!" She pulled the shades hard and let them pop to the tops of her windows, and danced on one foot, then the other as she raced into her clothes. "Happy birthday to me! Happy birthday to me! I've got a special lady, and she's gonna marry me!"

Jackie lived on the west side of the city and Mike hummed, sang, and tapped her fingers all the way there. Even when she saw Rachel in front of Jackie's house she couldn't make herself stop smiling. She pulled up to the curb and gallantly went to the passenger side to open the door. She didn't acknowledge Rachel because Rachel was obviously trying to ignore her, but she did nod to Jackie's landlady as she waited for everyone to finish talking. When Jackie finally got in the car, Mike stopped herself from holding the door too long or acting too macho. When she got behind the wheel, she cocked her head and smiled to make sure Jackie was with her, and the smile she always seemed to wait for was the best present she could get.

"Are you ready to go hug spring?" Mike asked.

Jackie didn't really look at her and Mike assumed she was a little nervous. After all, they had been friends for some time, but this was a date.

She drove out of the city and into the hills still bruised from their winter beating. She drove further south and into Letchworth State Park, where the river was flowing freely and the tulips at the inn were almost in bloom. Jackie barely said a word but seemed to be enjoying the ride.

"It's not quite beautiful yet," Mike said.

"It is. I always liked it out here. My kids live with their father about twenty miles from here."

Mike gently touched Jackie's hand on the seat next to her and tried to squeeze it a little to show her she understood, but Jackie pulled it away.

"Sorry," Mike said sheepishly.

"Rachel says I should flee from you," Jackie announced. "She told me and my landlady, Mary, how bad it's been for her. She said I should run from you as fast as I can."

Mike carefully slowed the car, pulled to the side of the road, and turned off the engine. She hadn't expected an attack so soon, and after all she'd been to Rachel, her words were particularly hurtful.

"Rachel's allowed to say and do whatever she has to," Mike said calmly. "She hurts, and people in pain say painful things." She looked Jackie straight in the eye. "But she doesn't hurt from me. It was Rachel's expectations that hurt her the most, unrealistic expectations. I never promised her a lifetime and I think she knows that."

Jackie looked at Mike fearfully, as if others' words were more important to her than Mike's.

"If you want to run, do it now." Mike's anger at a community that wouldn't let her love peacefully forced the words from her heart. "Do it now," she said louder, "before I can't see my heart anymore or save it from drowning. I already love you more than I can handle, and it's only going to get deeper."

She put her hands gently but firmly on Jackie's shoulders. "I don't want you if you're going to leave me, and I'd make damn sure I wasn't here now if I was going to leave you, but I can't promise we'll never hurt or cry or feel like running away. If it's real, we'll do it all. If it's real, we'll make love and make it better. If it's even close to what love is supposed to be, we'll be the highest and lowest we've ever been, hurt more than we thought we could, and feel happiness only angels know."

Her voice and hands shook as she tearfully looked into Jackie's eyes. "If you're going, go now. Or never go again."

Jackie looked into her lap and seemed almost prayerful as Mike lovingly rubbed her shoulders and arms. When their eyes met again, Mike drew her closer.

"I say we'll try," Jackie whispered.

"I say I love you." Mike kissed her urgently, softly, hopefully, and no bruise or scar or memory could lessen the depth of her love or the power of her trust.

Mike showed Jackie the power of the Genesee River and told her stories of the people who once lived there. They shopped at antique stores, listened to music, and held hands on a hill while the deer searched for spring food.

"Why are you going this way?" Jackie asked when Mike headed her car east.

"You said you used to live out here, right?"

"Yes, but I don't want..."

"So let's drive by," Mike interrupted. "Maybe we can catch a glimpse of your kids."

"No! Turn around! I really don't want to go anywhere near that house."

"You love them, and they'll always love you. We'll just drive by."

When they got to the hill Jackie had once called home, Mike slowed to peek through the windows of the house. "I see a girl, kind of tall. It looks like she's setting the table in the dining room. Jackie? Is that one of your daughters?"

Jackie crouched in fear behind Mike's body.

"C'mon. They're not paying any attention."

"It's my oldest, Laura. Oh, please, can we leave?"

Mike heard her plea but also saw her curiosity and longing. She wanted Jackie to make some kind of peace with her past, and she almost hoped one of the kids would see her. She made a U-turn and drove by again so Jackie could look from her window, but again Jackie crouched in the seat and dug her nails into Mike's arm.

"I'd die if they saw me," she said. "Laura looks so big. And I don't see Lisa or Joey."

"They're around. And I bet they wish they could peek at you, too."

"That's enough, Mike. I can't take any more."

Mike stepped on the gas and sped down the hill with new hope. She knew she and Jackie could work through old pain and survive, and she knew someday Jackie would see her children again.

They stopped for a quick dinner and then went to Jackie's before Mike's meeting. The landlady and her partner were waiting on the inside stairs like parents checking out their daughter's first date. Mike was wary of their imposing interest.

"Do they always wait?"

"Oh, yes. They feel like they took me in after I left my husband, and now they watch my every move. They're just protecting me. Mary's the bigger one. Tilly's the friendlier one."

Mike already disliked them, especially Mary. She looked like a mother hen and acted like a jealous lover, and she had glared at Mike when Rachel sounded her warning.

"Well, there's no one here now but us." Mike took each of Jackie's hands and lightly kissed it. "I want to make love to you—"

"I say no," Jackie interrupted.

"—but I really can't," Mike continued. "I don't want to rush. So, thanks for the day." She kissed Jackie's hands again and put them around her neck. "Kiss me good-bye." She lightly kissed Jackie's neck and hugged her. "And let me see you again soon so I can go on living." She looked into Jackie's eyes and pressed her lips against hers.

❑ ❑

The tenant meetings were getting more tense as the land-lords increased their threats of eviction. Every meeting became a shouting match and lasted longer than the one before.

"We can't quit now." Mike tried to calm everyone, and raise awareness in the community so that the landlords would also feel more pressure. She organized pickets and almost wept when the women with canes and walkers joined her on the sidewalk.

"This is one reason not to quit," she told a reporter. "These people are on rent control, a special program in effect since World War II. Their rents are stabilized until they move or die. The landlords often stage burglaries and harassment to terrify the older people into moving so they can double or triple the rent for someone new. One of our demands involves special security for them."

Jackie didn't join her at any meetings or pickets, but Linda showed up whenever she wasn't working and some-times kept Mike up longer than she wanted to be. She often asked Mike about the "new lady," and Mike often felt bad that Jackie wasn't around to be introduced.

"We're just a weekend thing right now," Mike explained, somewhat embarrassed.

"Aha! So she won't sleep with you, right? She says no and then keeps you coming back, right?"

"She's not ready," Mike said.

"Is she over twenty-one?"

Mike nodded.

"Is she a virgin?"

Mike shook her head.

"Then she's ready. She's just afraid she's going to fall in love with you. Since when are you afraid of tackling that? Go after her, for Christ's sake. What the hell's the matter with you?"

Mike tapped her fingers nervously on the table and then drew pretend circles. "I can't rape her. If she doesn't want me, she doesn't."

"I don't believe it. If you love her, show her. It's that simple. You want me to show you how?"

"No. No, not right now. I know how. I just don't want her to run away."

"Better to find out now than later."

❏ ❏

Mike waited until the summer breezes were perfect and she was rested enough to be as charming as possible, then she invited Jackie out for dinner, a walk, and a cool conversation on the floor of her apartment.

"I thought you'd like it here because it's so much more open than your house," Mike said, placing pillows on the floor. "I don't know how you can stand only three windows."

"Only one of them opens. But it's the best I can do. And Mary and Tilly take good care of me."

Mike opened the big French doors that led to the balcony and presented the tops of trees to Jackie. "All yours, from me to you."

She slid onto the floor next to Jackie and rested on one elbow to face her. "You don't really need Mary and Tilly, you know. You'd be better on your own, heeding your own heart and mind."

"That's your opinion. They give me good advice."

"Let's not fight," Mike said quickly. "The night's too nice and too short." She leaned forward and kissed Jackie passionately but with pauses to allow any second thoughts.

"I don't know if I want this," Jackie said as she kissed her back. "I think I should say no."

They kissed with kisses that don't seem to breathe and never want to end.

"I want you, honey," Mike whispered. "Not just tonight, not just a little."

"I want you, too, Mike."

"Take me then. You've got all of me. Marry me. Let me love you, give to you, grow old with you."

"I don't know," Jackie gasped as Mike dragged her fingers up her thigh. "I should say no."

"Say yes." Mike kissed her neck and trailed down to her shoulders. The breeze through the door caused Jackie to shiver as the wetness from Mike's tongue drew rivers on her body. "Say yes. Let me roam your body and feel all of you."

170

"No, Mike." Jackie moved her body slightly away from Mike's touches, but only slightly. "But I do want you. I do."

Mike slowly moved down between Jackie's legs and cupped her mouth to blow hot breath through Jackie's stockings. "Say yes."

Mike slid her fingers inside the elastic of the nylons and Jackie's hands grabbed her fingers. Mike moved her face up and down and back and forth between Jackie's legs, savoring every angle, every scent, and Jackie began to move with her.

"Say yes," Mike repeated. Jackie's fingers circled Mike's hands and slowly she helped Mike remove her nylons. Mike peeled them to Jackie's ankles while moving her mouth up and around the cool flesh of Jackie's inner thighs. "Say yes."

"Oh, Mike. I don't want to get hurt."

"Neither do I. We have to trust each other."

She let her hands open Jackie to her, but still she wouldn't take her love.

"Say yes, Jackie. Say yes and we'll find a way."

"It's so hard."

"I know, I know." Mike snaked her body back up on top of Jackie's and held her while she whispered in her ear. "Nothing's easy, honey. I have to trust you, too. We'll be okay as long as we stick together."

"But my friends say—"

"Shh. Listen to your heart. Listen to your soul. Listen to the angels."

"Yes. Yes, yes, yes. Oh, God, yes!"

Mike's happiness made her eyes fill with tears as she savored the woman beneath her. She explored every angle, every dent, every line that led to Jackie's heart and the salt from her body etched a path into Jackie's being.

❏ ❏

"I shouldn't visit you anymore, Linda. Lunch, maybe, but we can't be as close as we have been."

"Aha! So you got laid!" She looked at Mike with a sneer and a twinkle in her eye. "She musta been awfully good."

"Why do you always have to reduce everything to sex? I'd love this woman without it if I had to."

171

"Good thing you don't have to. You'd be impossible to live with. Did Ana talk to you yet?"

"No, why? I haven't spoken to her in weeks."

"Her parents are coming and she wants them to stay in your apartment. She asked me to take you in for the week they're here."

"And when was she going to tell me?"

"Don't know, my dear. That's between you and her."

Mike paced Linda's kitchen. Of course Ana assumed everything would be okay. Mike owed Ana's parents a favor: her hospitality in return for theirs. It was culturally correct.

"I could stay at Jackie's. I think."

"Better ask," Linda said. "And quick. They're coming in ten days. And I don't mind if you stay here, especially since it's so close to home. I'll be workin' anyway."

"Jackie would mind. I think the community has her on the defensive. She doesn't trust me."

"Oh, brother, are you in trouble." Linda lit a cigarette and shook her head in disbelief. "How the hell did you get mixed up with someone who doesn't trust you? With all the people you have buzzin' around your hive? You're going to make this woman crazy."

"She knows I need people. She's not like that. She just doesn't know who you are, that's all."

"Then introduce me."

"No!" Mike spun around fiercely, surprised at her own reaction. "I mean, she might think ... I don't want her to think that..."

"Oh, I get it. You don't want her to know we ever fucked around, right?"

Mike nodded, ashamed. "She'd think we still were. Her friends would tell her that. I don't really have anyone who's just a friend. Even Ana is a problem. As long as she knows I won't leave Jackie for her, we can't be friends. And if Jackie's friends take one look at you, they'll tell her to run."

"Thanks loads."

"I mean you'd be a threat to them. You're beautiful, not in their precious community, and different."

"So, does this mean you and me call it quits, or what?"

"No. You're too important to me. If you had trouble with Jackie, I'd tell you to fuck off, but you don't, so we can stay friends."

Linda put her arms around Mike's neck. "You know, little Mike, you make your life awfully complicated. If this woman doesn't trust you now, she's going to distrust you even more later."

Mike kept the embrace friendly and thought about what Linda was saying. She hated Jackie's friends for poisoning her with thoughts about what *could* happen. She wished Jackie was strong enough not to listen, but she had heard it many times already. Every time Mike left Jackie's, the phone rang. Once or twice, Mike heard Jackie telling whatever friend was on the other line that she wasn't sure where Mike was going or didn't know if Mike meant what she said.

"I'll make her trust me," Mike said. "If she loves me, she'll listen."

❏ ❏

Jackie wasn't ready for Mike to spend an entire week at her house when Ana's parents arrived. The apartment was tiny and boxy, and they were still trying to know each other while cleaning up past problems. So Mike split her time between Linda's and the West Side. She was busy playing host and dealing with landlords, so she and Jackie didn't have too much time together. Then, the day before she was supposed to reclaim her apartment, Jackie wrote her a note.

Dear Mike,
    I think we should stop seeing each other. I don't feel good about our relationship and I don't want either of us to get hurt. Sorry. Jackie.

"I don't get it," Mike said to Linda tearfully. "I have to talk to her, find out why."

"Don't say a word," Linda commanded. "This woman is obviously insecure. Someone's making her believe everything you do is no good. Just keep your mouth shut and let her come back to you. She will. She thinks she wants out because she's not the one doing the thinking."

Mike didn't really believe what Linda was saying, but she was so hurt, so devastated by Jackie's note, that she was unable to do anything but cry and pace and worry and cry some more. For three days, she kept her silence; for three nights, she raged at all people who do their best to destroy what's good or kind or loving. She wanted to shake Jackie until all doubts planted by her friends and her past were gone. Then, maybe she could see that Mike was also her friend and deserved to be listened to.

"Thanks for being here for me," she told Linda. "I owe you one."

"You owe me more than one, but we'll let it go for now. If that woman of yours doesn't call by the end of the week give her up."

"Right."

Mike knew she'd never give up on Jackie. Even if they never spoke again, she'd continue to love her. She had made a pact with the trees and the stars, a promise she would never break, and nothing Jackie could do would ever change that.

Two days later, Jackie called. "This was too easy," she said to Mike. "So it doesn't feel like it should have happened. I guess I just got cold feet."

"Are you gonna marry me, or not?"

"Yes."

"How about Labor Day weekend?"

"How about Philadelphia where my sister is?" Jackie answered.

"Fine. How about dinner?"

"My house or yours?"

"Yours. Mine is a mess. And we need to talk about that too. About making some place ours."

"I'm ready to talk," Jackie said warmly. "And I do love you."

❏ ❏

They set the wedding date and ordered plane tickets and talked about what they'd wear and tried to find rings special enough, but finally decided to have them made. It was fun and scary and exciting, and to Mike, it was the culmination of thirty-two years of searching. Marriage was the answer, and Jackie was the one. Their rings would bind them; their vows would intercede in times of trouble.

The landlords, seeming to sense Mike's inattentiveness to the tenants, chose the end of June for the final struggle in court.

They called Mike at work to try to force her into settling outside of court.

"Do the right thing," they said. "Otherwise people could get hurt."

She met with lawyers, held mock trials, and constantly reassured her neighbors. The landlords' threats continued, and an unmarked car tried to run her down as she crossed the street. Men in suits showed up at her door asking questions about her friends, her past, her acquaintances in the building. Once, she saw two men on the corner watching her window. She ran to her dresser to retrieve the picture from Chile. She was sure one of the spies was the same man in the photo. She wondered about her landlords' connections with the government.

"You will always be watched," Ana told her. "The FBI, the CIA. You have been in the military. You've been to my country. You were part of the women's movement, a movement much like a revolution in this country. And you are gay. The men you saw are all the same, all part of the same institutions."

Always, she returned to Jackie's arms and the serenity of their embraces. She barely spoke about the pressure or the threats; she didn't want anything to destroy what they had.

As the court date drew nearer, the threatening calls to Mike's job increased. She found herself taking on more work to convince her boss he could count on her.

The day before the trial, she decided to spend time with Amalia, special time to make up for lost conversation and missed embraces. They played and colored and watched *Little House on the Prairie* and Mike tried to show her she'd always love her.

"Here, Mike. I think you should take this."

Amalia handed Mike a flat little package hand-wrapped in tissue paper and marked with a heart.

"I wanted to keep it," Amalia said. "But I think you need it now."

Mike untied the string, peeled away the tape from the fragile package, and smiled a choked smile as she smoothed the picture of her and Amalia on the swing.

"I wanted you to know I didn't move away," Amalia said strongly.

"Neither did I, squirt." She pressed the picture into her shirt pocket and bent over to kiss Amalia's forehead. "You're getting to be quite a beautiful person." She glanced at Ana with a sadness the two of them would always know and then left to prepare herself to face the judge.

❏ ❏

Jackie told her to call as soon as she knew anything, then tenants filed into cars and buses bound for the courthouse. Mike met alone with attorneys and was considered the main plaintiff. The landlords brought four lawyers and mingled with building inspectors and judges as Mike's lawyer met in the judge's chambers. After three hours, she was motioned into the chamber as her neighbors sat anxiously, fearfully, on the benches outside.

"C'mon in, Ms. Landetti, and have a seat."

Mike entered the room confidently, trying to show the judge she wasn't afraid of him. She was right and she knew it and she tried to trust that the legal system would recognize the tentants' rights.

The landlords entered from another door and stood rigidly in their dark suits as the judge studied the papers in front of him.

"Is my attorney coming in?" Mike asked.

"No lawyers," said the judge. "We're going to keep this between me and you."

Mike eyed the landlords and felt some of her confidence leave her. "Are they staying?"

"The have a right to know what I'm going to say, Landetti. They own those buildings you live in. They let you live there and do whatever else it is you do there."

He straightened the papers before folding his hands in ultimate power.

"This is the deal, Landetti. You have twenty-three people out there who are on rent control. You have two people getting married and one with a baby on the way. There's a friend of yours across the hall who might be into drugs and one we think might be an illegal alien. Your gay friend, Jim, is no angel, and the couple next door to you are pretty upset about some of the noises coming from your apartment. So, here's what you're going to do. You will resign as president of this stupid association effective at three today and will turn over all of the escrow money. You will vacate your apartment by July 15th and not return to the premises for one year. Your association will never assemble again, and you will speak to no one about tenants' rights."

Mike looked at him and almost laughed at the absurdity of his demands. "You're kidding, right? We'll go to trial, a jury trial, and prove we're right. You can't just take the law into your own hands and tell me what I can and can't do! I'm no criminal."

"You're right," the judge answered smugly. "What I called this was a deal. If you don't do everything I've just outlined for you, I will personally prosecute every one of those people waiting for you out there. All the old ladies will be off rent control and on the street. The couple with the baby will be on the street. Your gay friend will be behind bars. Am I making myself clear?"

Mike felt the bars closing around her. Rage filled her body as her face reddened and she prepared to strike.

"Don't do anything stupid, Landetti. You're planning some kind of wedding, too. I wouldn't want you spending your wedding night in jail. Do we have a deal or not?"

Mike walked from the chambers and faced the bench as she had been instructed to do. The landlords smirked on her right; the tenants gasped behind her.

"Michaelene Landetti. You have agreed to return all money with interest and to relinquish your presidency of the Main-Jewel Tenants Association. You have further agreed to disband said association and restrain from further assembly. You have also relinquished all rights to your apartment and agreed to vacate the premises eighteen days from today. Say to the court you will."

177

Mike's anger heaved inside of her and all of her pride rose to her eyes. She could feel the incredulous stares behind her, and her heart wept for their defeat. She hadn't known the extent of corruption or power in Buffalo. She had made people believe in the law, in her, and in themselves, and in one mighty swoop of the judge's gavel, it would all be destroyed. But what choice was there?

"Answer the court. Say you will."

She answered, "I will," and felt her attorney wince.

"The court will record said agreement."

❏ ❏

Mike crouched in the hallway with her head buried in her hands as, one by one, the tenants pled their cases with the judge. He had promised not to prosecute and Mike waited through the afternoon to make sure he kept his end of the bargain. As long as she did what she was told, the tenants would get needed repairs and be able to live peacefully. They still wouldn't have security, but they'd have a place to live.

Jackie came as soon as she could and led Mike to a far corner, where she tried to console her. They couldn't touch or cry or even act very close, but Jackie's presence was the only truth, the only life Mike could feel.

❏ ❏

As she packed and moved, Mike felt the chilling silence of all who lived near her. They would never know the truth. She would never be able to tell them they had really won the fight.

Jackie agreed to take her in, and Mike had to face the fact that she would be living in someone else's house, a different space, a place she couldn't call her own. Jackie did her best to clear half of the tiny closet and two drawers in the dresser. She worked hard to make Mike's furniture central to the square, dark living room and to give the black chair a place of honor near the stereo. The wedding plans kept Mike from running away or feeling insane. She still had her job and was starting to catch up on past-due bills. She'd earn more by working harder, and they'd save for a place they could both call home.

❏ ❏

They arrived in Philadelphia on September 4th with rings and smiles. Jackie's sister made her apartment a small chapel and lined the hallway and living room with candles of all shapes and sizes. A friend who was once a priest donned his robes and greeted the couple at the altar. A gay man stood next to Mike and acted as best man. An ex-nun was in charge of the music. There were no other guests, no friends who approved.

Mike stood proudly in her rented tuxedo. She clasped the hand of the woman she would vow to love until death as the priest gave a blessing and read from the Bible.

"You have made my heart beat faster, my sister, my bride; you have made my heart beat faster with a single glance of your eyes, with a single strand of your necklace."

Mike's heart followed the priest's cadence, and her hand melted into the touch of her bride's. She watched Jackie as the blessings continued and cherished the smile, the softness of her skin, the sweetness of her. The flickering candles made the room look like a highway somewhere between heaven and earth, and Mike realized the utter beauty of this ritual denied to so many. Silently she thanked Sharon for being the first to truly open her heart; quietly she forgave Ana for being the first to truly destroy it.

The priest continued, "Do not urge me to leave you or turn back from following you; for where you go, I will go, and where you lodge, I will lodge. Your people shall be my people, and your God, my God. Where you die, I will die, and there I will be buried."

No earthly power could contain the brilliance of Mike's love. No man or woman could equal it, no judge overturn it, no distance erase it, no posse destroy it.

She placed the ring on Jackie's finger and spoke from the deepest parts of her heart. "With this band of molded silver, this ring with no beginning and no end, I commit myself to you before God and family. May we never have to test its strength. May it forever mold to our joined hands and remind us of our bond and our love, even after death."

They kissed and danced and cried and laughed and celebrated a new life. Philadelphia's gay bars became their reception halls; beer, the champagne. They basked in the joy reflected on the faces of strangers and danced with those few who truly felt their love was real.

When they arrived back in Buffalo, Mike wanted to run from house to house telling everyone about her marriage; to share it, brag about it, make it last.

Cuddled on the couch, she and Jackie played with the rings that now adorned their fingers. "I think we should have a reception here," Mike said. "Lesbians don't get the chance to celebrate weddings very often. We should invite everyone we can think of, friend or foe, and let them enjoy something special."

Jackie was nervous. She knew Mike's reputation and how badly she was judged. "Maybe just a little party would be better, Mike. There are a lot of people who don't agree with marriage."

"I don't think I've ever known a dyke who didn't want to be married in some way," Mike argued. "Even if a lot of people don't like me, I'm married now. I can't be labeled a home-wrecker or a cheat. Maybe some people will decide it's okay to be friends again."

They bought formal invitations and mailed them the night before the annual fall dance. It was Mike's first chance to show off a little in the community she had grown away from, but she was nervous and afraid as she chose a corner and held Jackie's hand. Jackie's friends seemed willing to accept whatever made her happy, but they were Jackie's friends. Mike needed people from her portion of the community to accept the marriage, too. She didn't strut, smile too widely, or dance in the middle of the floor. Instead, she sat in the glow of their commitment and relished their togetherness.

One of the "leaders of destruction" approached them, smiling, and Mike instinctively placed part of her body in front of Jackie to defend her.

"Jackie! I got your invitation today."

"Oh, good. That means everyone did, I guess."

"Frankly, I was surprised. Especially because it was you. Needless to say, we won't be there. We just can't support something like this. And with Mike, of all people."

Mike was stunned. Her heart cried out, "How dare you? What right do you have? How can you, a person who calls herself sister and friend, judge us for loving as deeply as we can?" She squeezed Jackie's hand to tell her not to listen, not to mind, not to react. These people weren't family. Strangers in Philadelphia had kissed them and cried with joy, but not in Buffalo. These people were divided, weak, afraid to accept change, afraid to enjoy happiness, afraid to forgive.

"C'mon, honey," Mike said. "We'll dance the night away and go home, to our home, and make love until there's no more love to make."

The following Saturday, Mike and Jackie donned their armor and readied the house for their reception. They hadn't received many responses, but there were hushes and glances from every direction of the city and they knew the house would be full.

"They're coming because they're curious," Jackie said. "I don't feel comfortable with this whole thing."

Maggie didn't come, nor did Ana, Leslie, Rachel, Cassie, Adrian, Linda, or Marge. Jackie's friends stayed close beside her and a few people brought gifts, but many came in costume to mock the ritual they said belonged to straight people, and many came to whisper or offer opinions about whether or not there should have been a marriage.

When it was over, the woman Mike loved so dearly shook and cried with embarrassment and pain. Mike vowed to never again give any of herself to the Buffalo community.

"Let 'em rot in hell and destroy each other," Mike cried as she held Jackie in her arms. "It'll all come back at them. Someday they'll look for the same acceptance, the friendship, the credit for doing what's right or good, and it won't be there. Someday they'll be old, sick, or lonely, and there'll be no friends to see them through."

Mike waited until Jackie finally fell asleep before secretly releasing her own sorrow. She had wanted acceptance so badly. She so much wanted her and Jackie to be loved again, enjoyed as they once were, included in things only lesbians do. She hated feeling alone. She raged at those who hurt her lover and said they did it because they cared. She raged at her parents for leaving her alone so long ago. And she cursed all people who ever judged loving as wrong.

"We have so much to go through," she whispered to Jackie as she slept. "Stay strong, dear woman."

She wished they could move away, maybe to California, maybe anywhere but here. She wondered if she could find work, and she worried that Jackie wouldn't follow.

❏ ❏

"Sorry, Mike," her boss said on Monday. "I have to close up, lay everybody off. Been in business thirty-five years and never seen the economy like this. The whole city is falling apart. Sorry."

Mike called Jackie at work and stoically told her the news. "I've got two weeks and that's it. No job and no money."

As she listened to Jackie's pained silence, her strength drained away from her, and her butch pride, her human dignity, seemed to run with her tears.

"I can't believe I'm crying at work," Mike said. "I'm like a big crybaby lately."

"Don't worry," Jackie said. Mike heard her almost call her "honey" and knew others must be close to her phone. "You'll find something. We'll make it. I'll meet you at home. Our home, remember?"

"I remember. I love you, sweetheart. No one ever loved anyone as deeply as I do you."

When the two weeks were over, Mike once again faced the unemployment line. She wrote her parents to give them her new address and visited Linda while Jackie was working to talk about options, share the pain of feeling poor, and feel the kinship of a working-class woman.

"I'm going to California," she told Jackie. "I'll take a driveaway car and be there in three or four days. If I find a job, you have to promise to follow."

"I don't really want to, Mike. I'm not ready. But I'll go with you if you ask me to."

Mike drove the tortuous three thousand miles alone and tried to draw renewed strength from the mountains near Flagstaff and the desert beyond. She couldn't ask Jackie to move. Leslie had wanted to move when Mike wasn't ready, and the conflict of self versus commitment had helped destroy their relationship. She couldn't ask Jackie to give up what little she had to take a chance on another beginning.

When she reached the coast, she felt divided and conquered. She needed work and friends and family. She needed to flee the overpowering, destructive forces of Buffalo. But she needed Jackie more. She climbed mountains and walked the streets of San Diego and L.A. searching for work and probing for answers. She removed her ring and caressed the whiter circle beneath it as she prayed to a God she felt had forgotten her. Home was the only answer she heard. She'd go home to Jackie and find a better way. They'd face the winter together and make a path they both could walk on. She didn't call or leave a number so Jackie could reach her, but sent a letter timed to arrive the day she'd get back home.

My dear sweet woman,
    I'm home now, near you and with you, alive again, if only for a moment. Seize it! Grab it! Know how much I love you and am willing to endure. Don't give me too much. Don't give so much of yourself that you expect me to give more. And see me as I really am. Not the husband you married once; not the man who slapped your body and punched your heart. Know my past, my faults, my terrible fear of losing you, and the incredible depth of my love for you. If you show me you're giving too much, I'll pull away to set you free. If you show me you're too needy, I'll be absent when you need me most and make you find your own strength. Our love will be hell, but not for long. We'll ride the tides, bear the pain, and know each other more than any two should be allowed, but we'll have the greatest gift, the deepest love, the truest friendship.

She returned to Jackie a person in turmoil, a woman afraid of having nothing to give, a friend fearful of their differences but in love enough to trust.

She shined her car, looked for work, and picked up Jackie every day at five. Together, they opened their home to all who needed friendship or peace or just a place to be.

Together, they cried when the pressure of working or not having work seemed too great; separately, they sobbed when they had no more to give.

Unemployment turned to welfare and Mike suffered the agony of the new poor, the labeled people. Her worn clothes matched the rips and tears in her spirit. More and more, she lived as she felt the world wanted her to.

Jackie asked her to try, to make dinner for her, to clean, to do something to give her life meaning. She heard and she tried, but her natural resistance to change and the falseness of her pride made her strike out and deny that anyone cared.

She went to Linda and asked her for her help.

"Before it's too late," Mike pleaded. "I don't know where to go, what to do. I feel like I no longer know how to survive. Jackie works and work makes her crazy, but it's her money that gives us shelter and puts food on the table. I can't live like that. I need to give. I need the power that comes with providing."

"You're a mess, little Mike. Toughen up. If she's with you, she's with you, and she's obviously willing to go through it."

"You don't understand. I feel guilty living there. I feel guilty when her head hurts from working and I have no strength to make it better. I run so I don't feel helpless. I hide so she won't know what a nothing I've become."

When Linda couldn't give her answers, she swallowed what pride she had left and went to Ana.

"It's your time, Mike. You began this process long before your marriage, and it's time for the final skin to be shed. You have all those scars, all that bleeding, and finally it's coming to the surface. You have to go with it, let it take you where you have to be. If you fight it, it will destroy you."

Mike sobbed in Ana's cautious arms. "But it's destroying us, me and her together and each of us separately."

"Her skin is her own, Mike. You love her, and she knows that. She feels it, even if she doesn't admit how much. Your love is making her shed her skin, too, and she'll also lose if she fights it."

Mike lost all reason, all memory of each long day. Each hour was a maze of nothingness and idleness and contained confusion. She knew Jackie was distancing herself and knew it was for her own survival, but she couldn't fight it, couldn't respond to it.

Sometimes, when they had made love and felt each other's pain melt away for the night, Mike would feel a breath of hope, a hint of something better. For a day or a week, she'd be filled with energy while she searched for work and contacted old friends. But then the rejections would begin again and Jackie would need her, expect her to be there, and Mike's heart would ache from trying to be all she couldn't be.

The crash was loud. When Mike heard it, she knew without looking that someone had struck the final blow. Her car was crushed. The hit-and-run driver had sped away, leaving only a trickle from his radiator.

Jackie, just home from work, had seen the crash, but Mike couldn't look at her or go to her for comfort. She had lost her car, her horse, her last hope for recovery, her last hope of getting a job. She didn't expect Jackie to understand her grief or her need. Jackie rode buses and had been a housewife for twenty years. Her job was more a beginning step to a working life. But Mike was a working-class butch with muscles and graying hair. Her last chance for freedom, power, and security was shattered into tiny blue pieces.

She knew now how her father must have felt when he lost his business and had to depend on his wife for security. She knew now how his pride must have suffered, how his rage struck at all he cared for.

"Fuck you!" she yelled at Jackie instead of the world that had hurt her. "What do you know about being on welfare or losing friends or being judged when you shouldn't be?" She accused Jackie of pulling away and distancing herself when it was Mike who was running. "You don't say you love me or need me. You just say you don't feel married or together. Try being me for a while. You run to your landlords every time we argue and call Philadelphia to talk behind my back. You want out, right? You can't stand it that I'm not who I used to be. You want out? Go! I can't leave."

"I call Philadelphia to save our relationship," Jackie said calmly. "Because I don't want out, I don't want to leave."

Oh, God, how Mike loved her. She ached to hold her and buy her flowers and let Jackie know how wonderful she was, but she hurt and she was scared. She was too poor to buy flowers. She hated herself for loving when she shouldn't have.

"I'm sorry. I'm sorry you ever loved me," Mike sobbed. "I should have stayed away, left you alone until all of this crap that makes up my history was solved and healed. I'm sorry."

"I could have stayed away, too," Jackie comforted. "But I love you."

When the phone rang for Jackie, Mike grabbed it first to tell whoever was intruding to leave them alone, let them be alone so they could try to love each other again. But the intruder was new, an attorney from downtown, and his message was one neither of them could handle.

"Your ex-husband is suing you for child support, six hundred dollars a month, and his case is strong enough to win."

"Oh, Mike. What do I do now? I can't pay. I can't win. I can't bear to see my children in a courtroom and have them think I don't care enough to support them."

Mike cradled Jackie in her arms and tried with all her might to find the right words, the right feelings. "I want to go with you, to be with you, support you. Nothing else matters now. You'll get through this and beat it and your kids will know you love them."

"You can't go, Mike. If the other lawyer sees you, or the judge sees you with me, they'll know. They'll accuse me of things because I'm a lesbian. They'll make me pay more than I can afford. It could make things worse."

"Oh, honey, please don't do this. It's the only chance I have to do something for you that matters, something you need that I can give."

"No, Mike. You can't."

Mike paced and waited as each day in court became another, as the days turned to weeks. When winter turned to spring, she slowly began to breathe.

"I think we'll make it," she told Linda over coffee. "I'm going to quit looking for bosses and find a way to support myself. Even if Jackie loses and has to pay child support, I'll find a way to help her. She'll need me more than ever and that seems to make me think straighter."

"Give her space to deal with it if she loses, kiddo. Otherwise all the shit she feels for the ex-husband is going to come right at you."

"She gives herself space. She closes up and sits alone, and I get lost. She'll be okay. If she'd just stay away from the social workers and landlords and think for herself, she'd be much stronger."

"Never met a social worker yet who didn't need therapy," Linda answered, smiling. "And as far as the landlords go, it sounds to me like the fatter one has a crush on Jackie and that's why she's always buzzin' around."

"She ever touches her, she's dead," Mike said assuredly.

❑ ❑

"It's over." Jackie stood in the doorway, notebook and tissues in hand. Her face was drawn and gray, her knuckles were peeled and red. "Two hundred a month, more than a third of what I make before taxes."

Mike went to her carefully. "Honey, we'll find a way. I'll find work somehow. The lousy bastard!"

"No, Mike. It's okay. I should have been there for those kids, and I ran away to protect them. Now I have to pay and that's fine, 'cause I love them."

Jackie's husband had gotten the house, the truck, the furniture, and the kids, and made three times more than she did. Mike was amazed that Jackie could somehow still feel responsible. It reminded her of her own mother telling her she had to leave home. In a way, she had protected Mike from her father's rage by abandoning her.

"They'll come back to you someday, honey. I know they'll come back. They'll understand why you left and that you didn't really leave at all."

❑ ❑

When spring turned to summer, Mike was beginning to feel stronger. She spent her days alone, writing in journals and continuing to scrape at old wounds and scars. She wrote about her childhood, people she remembered, highways she'd traveled, and places she'd been. She knew she wasn't done yet. She knew she had a lot more healing and pain to

187

face, but she felt better. She didn't run away from Jackie as often or hide from Jackie's need. She didn't yell at her anymore or accuse her or deny her. They were married and the first year had been hell, but they'd lasted and Mike had no regrets.

Jackie cuddled in Mike's arms on the couch and they talked about things that needed to be fixed in the house and places to go in the summer. Jackie was still distant and worn from all they'd been through, but Mike trusted her and loved her and tried to show her things were changing.

"You wanna do something special for our anniversary?" Mike asked. "Like maybe go to Philly?"

"I want our relationship to end, Mike."

"What?"

"It's not good for either of us. I've talked to people about it, and I want it to be over."

Mike was stunned into silence. Jackie had to be kidding or playing a game, or maybe testing Mike to see if she'd leave. What people had she spoken to? How could she want them to end right when they finally had a chance for a beginning?

"That's what you really want?" Mike asked. "That would make you happy?"

Jackie nodded and Mike still couldn't believe it. "C'mon. Let's go talk to some of these people you've spoken to. I want to see what they say about it."

They made the rounds of Jackie's friends, and the more they spoke the more Mike began to believe Jackie meant what she'd said. They had all known before Mike that a breakup was on the horizon. Mike hated them for allowing it to happen.

Mike and Jackie went home — to bed and lovemaking and tears and hugs. Jackie had made up her mind and intended to stick to it, but they still loved too deeply to stay away. They were best friends and they could only find comfort with each other, in each other's arms and in the knowledge that they were still loved.

Leaving each other made no sense to Mike. They had found what people always look for, and Jackie wanted to give it up. For days and weeks, Mike pleaded with Jackie to change her mind. Jackie asked her to move. She told Mike to go to Linda, but even Linda's friendship was no comfort. She couldn't put up with Mike's anger or crying or persistent questioning. Mike begged Jackie's friends to understand what they had done and make Jackie understand so they could renew their vows and stay together, but no one listened. She tried to call Philadelphia, but didn't have a number, so she wrote a letter pleading with them to help before it was too late. She left notes and letters and flowers and food and anything and everything she could think of to make Jackie know that she loved her more than life and would die for her if she asked. She told Jackie she'd change into anything and anyone she wanted if only Jackie would come back and try again.

When Mike accused Linda of being one of the reasons for the breakup, Linda responded by telling her to leave. "I'm not responsible for your mistakes or her insecurities," Linda said. "You want to cry about it and find excuses, go somewhere else."

Mike slept on Jackie's steps so she could be near her. She cried through the night, every night, shaking, screaming, pleading with God to help them stay together. But the fall turned colder, and so did Jackie. There was nowhere left for Mike to go.

"Dad? Michaelene." When she said her name and heard her father's voice she was no longer anyone she knew. Her uncontrolled sobs turned to screams and pleas. She begged her father to let her come home.

"I have no one," she cried. "Nothing. I need ... I need ... please, Dad, help me. I have to come home before I go crazy."

"Okay, honey, okay. Come home. Come home. We're here."

They cried together on the phone and Mike's heart exploded within her. "As soon as I can get there," she stuttered.

"Okay, honey. Don't worry. Everything will be okay. Come home."

After hanging up, she slumped to the floor and beat her fists into the wood until exhaustion overcame her. She was broken and lost and weaker than a child. She was old and too young and a butch who could no longer be proud.

When she was able, she stopped by Ana's to say good-bye. Ana couldn't help and didn't try, but Mike understood there was nothing she could do. She purposely didn't see Amalia. "I want her to remember me like I used to be. I don't want her to see the shell I've become."

She boarded the bus that followed the shore of Lake Erie and left the skyline of the city behind her. As the bus passed the bank where Jackie worked, Mike tapped three fingers against her heart and kissed the ring she would always wear.

❑ ❑

Dear Jackie,

I'm home now. Back where I started, back with the people who began my life. My father is now my counselor, my mother my companion, and as the leaves fall around me in the backyard that was once my stage, I let the trees be my lovers, the wind my friend.

You're everywhere. A snowy owl looks down on me or the sun blinks through a branch and my arms, so weighted at my side, reach for you and touch you and hold you so you can't run away. But you're not there, or so I'm told. You were only an illusion, a phase, no one I really knew. They say I should forget you, for my sake, and I say no. They say time will heal me, that no one is worth all this pain, but I say no. Love is worth it. Loving women is worth it. Nothing can destroy the part of me that sings every love song or dances much too close. Nothing can match the power of a woman's touch, a woman's smile, or a woman's tear. Butches are women who were made to love women, love them in spite of their weaknesses, love them for all their strengths, and love them deeper, harder, better than any man could.

I loved you. I loved you with every breath, every ounce of blood, and I'd stop at nothing to love you again. But now, as the leaves fall around me, I let the trees be my lovers, the wind my friend. My sister, my bride. I bid you farewell.

Love, Mike